One

The first time Jamie saw the boy, he was tied to a tree. She was in no way prepared for the sight, of him wrapped tight in old clothesline haphazardly wound and knotted, the rope soiled and stained where it had at some previous time curled on pulleys and grimed. He was remarkably still but for the snot that ran from his nose.

A half-dozen ragtag children formed an imperfect circle on the road's edge opposite the boy, clutching their schoolbooks covered in paperbag wrap to their chests. They swayed and milled and murmured nothing to one another and peered at the road as if by doing so they might conjure the schoolbus, but when Jamie's dog trotted toward them they broke rank, herded close to one another, the smaller children behind and grabbing at the waists of those who were taller. They faced the dog's approach with apprehension, in silence, but the dog passed them by without so much as a glance and then simply stopped before the boy and after a moment sat, so that she wondered at the sudden stillness of it all, the children and dog and boy motionless in haloed relief against the winter sun's bleak backdrop that allowed no shadows but gave their shapes a dark solidity she found disconcerting. They watched Jamie come on and remained as they were until the dog came off its haunches and took stance, let go a strangled sound resembling neither growl nor bark but rather a deep primordial howl, and at that instant the trussed boy bawled like a calf and the children shrieked and scattered. She began to run toward them but stopped abruptly and whistled, and the dog raced back, tail up and hackles raised, throwing its head to the side and looking over its shoulder the while, as if to keep the boy checked. She caught the dog up by its collar and got to the boy's side of the road, called out to the children, Don't be afraid, don't be afraid, but they distrusted the moment and did not recompose themselves into a group and instead wavered here and there at wary angles from one another until one of them yelled at the sound of the bus, and then they knotted together again, crossed the road as one. When the bus lumbered around the bend behind her and slowed, the children waved and shouted as though afraid it would not stop, but it did. As they scrambled onto it she yelled, Wait! *Wait!*, but they did not, and, still collaring the dog, Jamie half-ran toward the vehicle and slapped at the door just as it was closing. The door sighed

THE HOUSEKEEPER

Melanie Wallace

The Housekeeper

Harvill *Secker*
LONDON

Published by Harvill Secker 2007

First published in the United States by MacAdam/Cage in 2006

4 6 8 10 9 7 5 3

Copyright © Melanie Wallace, 2006

Melanie Wallace has asserted her right under the Copyright,
Designs and Patents Act 1988 to be identified as the author of this work

'Bobby's Girl' written and composed by Hank Hoffman and Gary Klein.
By permission of Edward Kassner Music Co. Ltd.

First published in Great Britain in 2007 by
HARVILL SECKER
Random House
20 Vauxhall Bridge Road
London SW1V 2SA

Random House Australia (Pty) Limited
20 Alfred Street, Milsons Point, Sydney,
New South Wales 2061, Australia

Random House New Zealand Limited
18 Poland Road, Glenfield,
Auckland 10, New Zealand

Random House (Pty) Limited
Isle of Houghton, Corner of Boundary Road & Carse O'Gowrie,
Houghton 2198, South Africa

The Random House Group Limited Reg. No. 954009

www.randomhouse.co.uk

A CIP catalogue record for this book is available from the British Library

ISBN 9781846550211

Printed and bound in Great Britain by Mackays of Chatham

for Peter, and for Claudia

open. That boy's tied, she cried, and the driver, a woman whose years had left her sorely worn, looked a tired look at the boy and then back at her. 'Course he is, she said.

〜

You should have left him there, Galen remarked.

I did.

But you untied him.

Jamie made no reply, and they sat in silence on Margaret's porch and watched the unkempt meadow tuft and spill into the spindly crabapple orchard that etched itself into the leaden sky grayshawling the far hill, and Galen rolled a cigarette and lit it. The smoke from the cheap tobacco he'd grown accustomed to curled blue, and its smell mingled with his own, that of oddly sweetscented sweat and hardwood fires, and with the stronger reek of the lemon wax she'd used on Margaret's floors, the tang of which still clung to her hands and to her shirt where she'd wiped them. The door gaped open behind them and beyond it the floors dried slowly in the bone-deep chill, and they did not go in. She shivered, thinking of the boy, and Galen peeled off his army jacket and put it over her shoulders and she shivered again, for the warmth and from his smell, and then they sat in the motionless positions of hunters in a blind until Galen rose and walked to the edge of the porch and there touched two fingertips to his tongue, pinched the lit end of the cigarette and extinguished it gingerly, crumbled the tobacco before exhaling a soft sigh and turning toward her.

He probably has more sense than you do, if he just stayed there.

What's that supposed to mean?

It means he probably knows why he was tied. That he was supposed to be tied. And that if he was untied and gone by the time whoever it was tied him came back for him, there'd be hell to pay.

Well he was there the last I looked.

Galen fought back a half-grin, contemplated the orchard so as to not meet her eyes. A fine-looking girl, Margaret once said to him, seeing him glance at Jamie as she walked past them toward the flowerbeds she'd been clearing—Margaret incisive as always, with those hooded intelligent eyes in her aged face, Margaret too incisive, too intelligent, to miss what Galen's look betrayed—lovely the way she holds herself, glides rather than walks, Margaret went on, but strangely wry beyond her years and maybe even beyond mine, not that she even knows what the word means. And then Galen and Margaret had watched her together, Galen feeling unabashed because complicit, until he turned to Margaret and commented, Well, maybe she's just matter-of-fact. Margaret pshawed then, told him: There's nothing matter-of-fact about that child. Why, she's been working for—with—me all summer, since end-May, and now it's almost Labor Day—and the only thing she's told me about herself is that she's someone things happen to. *Just*, Margaret corrected herself, someone things *just* happen to. And Galen had wondered then (as he wondered now) if Damon were one of those things that had happened to her, though Galen had told Margaret nothing of what little he knew from hearsay; but as he rose to go back to stripping her windowframes, Margaret stopped him with those intelligent eyes and in her incisive way acknowledged, though he'd mentioned nothing of the sort: It's good that you'll be coming by after I leave, even if the most you can do is see that she's getting by.

Not that he could tell, he now thought ruefully. Margaret had left in mid-September, it was almost Christmas, and Jamie hadn't told him anything more about herself than he already knew, which was little enough. They made small talk mostly—about her dog, a rangy, amber-eyed mongrel Margaret insisted must be a hybrid of the wild and the tamed, or about the raw, penetrating, relentless cold and the season, a winter drier than any Galen remembered, or about Margaret—and asked little of one another. Galen didn't pry. And never mentioning otherwise, betraying nothing to the contrary, Jamie left him little choice but to assume that things with her were as well as could be expected.

Jamie stood up, came toward him, stood close to him. Galen, she commented as she slipped out of his jacket and handed it to him, that sweater's seen better days. He studied the tattered weave with some seriousness and shrugged. Me too, he observed, then pulled on the jacket with feigned indifference, sauntered away from her closeness and went to the other end of the porch, rested a hand on the ancient wisteria that serpentlike and now barren wound itself around a column, tried to quell the surge within him. He stood that way for a long time.

It's getting late, he finally said. I've got to go.

Jamie walked over to him yet again, stood beside him yet again and yet again too close. Me too, she told him.

It'll snow. Finally. Lock up and get.

Soon as the floor's dry.

He nodded, allowed himself a glimpse of her almost hidden profile, took in her thick hair and its luster, resisted his urge to ask about Damon. C'mon, he said instead, and she stepped away, the dog before the stairs lifting its head from its paws and stretching into a stand as they approached it. Galen descended the porch and bent, roughed the dog's ears in farewell, straightened. See you, he told her, and she smiled, raised a curled hand, opened her fingers. And then he left as he always did, cutting up past the spring and pumphouse, not turning to look back before disappearing into the woods. She and the dog stood and surveyed his solitary going, and when he was no more she crouched at the door and tested the floor with the palm of one hand and told the dog to stay, then passed through the house, closing windows and interior shutters, casting darkness about her. The dog waited and sensed her moving within deep shadow until she reappeared and buttoned her thin jacket, pulled the door shut and locked it, slipped back into her shoes. When they set off the dog bounded beside her, begging rib thwacks and chest poundings, and Jamie obliged it both without breaking stride so that the two moved off in a tangle of motion that upset no balance until they reached the sumacs that edged Margaret's property, where the black shapes of startled crows rose skybound with cries and caws, the dog hard after them. She called the dog's name and it rushed back at her as though hellbent on collision, then feinted and circled about proudly before trotting on ahead. She followed, mindful of the freeze, thrusting her hands deep into her pockets and lowering her chin, hurrying down the mountain lane to the main road.

The main road was untrafficked, as it mostly was. It lay atop a makeshift route cut out two generations earlier for those people in the valley who lost everything they couldn't carry or cart away, lost everything to the watershed project that flooded their lands, vanished their homes and barns, sheds and fences, all they'd left behind: chests and chickencoops, corncribs, plows and harrows, shovels, worn-down shoes, worse-worn clothes, harnesses and hoes and horseshoes, feedbins, roughly sawed tables and handhewn chairs, barrelstoves, cords of seasoned wood, buttons, water troughs, dreams, their dead. They left on this road, going one way or the other, circumambulating the scalloped edge of the lands bought from them by the state for what they knew to be a pittance and over their objections, walking with their eyes on the ground, not acknowledging and returning no greetings from the crews fencing in the reservoir's boundaries, which stretched for nineteen miles along the side they walked. Those who chose to go in a southerly direction eventually reached a dam capped by a causeway at the reservoir's end; those who went north reached a bridge. The long causeway joined a road that led to a junction once (and still) called The Four Corners though the road back then (and even now) ended in a T-stop, where the one store most of them had ever entered sold everything they'd ever needed and served as a post office as well; the bridge over the river that fed into the reservoir's other end led to the route that took most of them along the same tributary and to dreary towns whose names—Dyers Corner, Tannersville, Foundry, Hatterstown, Bootsville, Sawmill—bespoke the lives of those who had come before them.

Jamie's grandfather and grandmother, who was not yet heavy with the child she was carrying, had been among those who walked toward the bridge, crossed it, went on. No one walked into the mountains, in which were scattered now long-abandoned or rarely used hunting cabins, bluestone quarries whose stone gave out some time before the valley vanished below the rising waters, here and there a wayward house within some random clearing. The valley's farmers were not mountain people, did not know the ways of mountains, could not envision eking out their livelihood tilling stonefields within an encroaching forest and living isolated from one another, unable to see their neighbors' homes, unable to raise livestock—for which there was no pasturage—and unable to be what they had been, which was the only thing they knew how to be, and unsure as to what they would become, other than knowing they would not become mountain people. And so most of them trudged, as Jamie's grandparents did, toward the mill-towns, losing one another to the places where they settled, a few moving in with distant relatives and most others renting cramped, shoddy rooms or houses better called shacks wherever they thought they might find work. But when they stopped at wherever it was they arrived, they found they couldn't make shift with what skills they had and discovered that the Depression had already laid waste to their dreams of learning new skills before they could even dream them. There was no work. Not for newcomers, not for many who had lived and worked in those towns all their lives. Most people found themselves having to survive any way they could, and by the skin of their teeth. Jamie's grandmother took in washing at Dyers Corner, as dreadfully poor and as like any of the other towns, and the child grew within her; the day after Jamie's mother was born Jamie's grandmother was back to boiling washwater and bluing whites and stringing lines with sheets and clothes not her own while her jobless husband uselessly reckoned, schemed, and pined, and even more uselessly sat and contemplated fate's fecklessness, thinking the while and for a long while thereafter that he would go mad.

Her grandmother and grandfather recrossed that bridge once, retraced their steps to the reservoir's edge only once, where they and others who were from there gathered on a foreordained day to gaze out over all that was now lost to them. Her grandparents never showed their only child those valley roads that cut away from the paved route Jamie now walked, some remnants yet studded with cobblestones or of packed dirt, all of them long ago forest-canopied and overgrown and leading nowhere but to the water's edge where they descended gently under the ice that in this season lay in splintered reams upon the reservoir's vast surface. There was nothing to flag them; the mailboxes Jamie passed— listing, leaning, tilted by the year-in, year-out force of snowplows and the uneven weight of banked snows— came later, after the reservoir, and belonged to those who at that time lived above the valley. On most, names could no longer be read, though across from them skewed poles bore the appellations—Richard's Hollow Road, Flagstone Road, Birch Lane, Quartz Creek Road, Loggers Way—of those lanes that climbed upward, opposite the reservoir, and deadended in slag heaps or stone walls or in hollows beyond which untended orchards, like Margaret's, bloomed sparsely each spring and dropped wormy fruit each fall, or lanes where cabins and hunting shacks and houses were once—and were sometimes still—lived in by those whose mailbox names had faded.

Jamie walked rapidly, trod the road without making a sound like a somnambulant gliding dreamlike and without language through the eerie twilight stasis, and she did not look up. The occasional, convulsive shrieks of bluejays tore through the day's end, and she thought of nothing except the brutal cold as she approached and passed the shabby trailer park that marked the imaginary boundary of what people simply and inexplicably called The Bend, the trailers weatherworn and stained and peeling, some uninhabited and others with wanton families who had even more wanton children, all with cinderblocks in lieu of steps, and most with refuse— empty cans and bottles, discarded carburetors and car batteries, broken ladders—strewn about their frontsides and dumped into the nearby marsh, which on spring and summer nights croaked with the same reptilian sounds as had given voice to all such wetlands for millennia and which now lay silent under a dull sheen of pearlgray ice. Jamie slowed beyond the trailers' thin lights, paused alongside the frozen marsh, for something about its glaciate deadness reminded her of the boy's eyes; and then she balled her chilled hands tighter in her pockets, looked about, realized the dog was nowhere in sight. She whistled once, twice, stamped her feet, waited,

went on past the stilted reeds and downed trees and rotting oildrums half-sunk in the frozen mire, quickened
her pace until she was breathless, clipped it to a quick
walk just below the junkman's place, which lay hidden
atop a careening hill whose sides were scarred by one
tangle after another of rusting bedsprings and demol-
ished iceboxes and bicycle rims and shredded tires and
wooden spokes and heaps of chickenwire and dented tin
washtubs and brokendown sideboards, tables, pie
hutches, the castoffs of innumerable disappeared families. A diffuse glow spilled from above, its source hidden
by the cliff overhang whereupon several generations of
junkmen and their offspring had lived and spawned in a
self-sufficient and mostly unaccountable way, their
descendents hermetic and isolated not so much by the
no-trespassing signs posted everywhere as by the
rumors of readied shotguns and lunatic albino children.

The dog did not appear, and Jamie moved toward
the middle of the road, unnerved by the way its shoulders were bleeding into the night, and hurried on until
she reached the tree where the boy had been tied. The
rope lay in tangles at its base, exactly as it had dropped
from her hands. As she contemplated it, unsure of the
import of what she had done or of what had become of
the boy, snowflakes drifted downward. Winter's heavens
kissing the ground.

∽

The house sat back from the road, and the light from within latticed ghostly white shadows onto the yard. The dog was already there, curled on the stoop, its fur shimmered with snow. As Jamie hurried toward it, unpocketing her hands and brushing the flurries from her hair, from her shoulders, the dog rose and shook itself.

Damon rocked back in his chair, a bottle of whiskey before him on the table, and raised his brimming shot glass in mock toast to her as she entered, said: Ah, my pizza parlor pickup. Jamie winced and without greeting him dragged a chair away from the table to the stove. Bare bulbs in two ceiling sockets spilled a harsh light that pooled where it hit. The house was dead cold and she did not take off her jacket but opened the oven door, fiddled with a knob, listened for the flame to catch. It whooshed when it did. She sat, flatpalmed the air, stared at her spread fingers, waited for the warmth.

Damon's chair scraped the floor when he came off it, and she turned her head at the sound, watched him fill the shot glass, drain it, set it on the table, screw the cap onto the whiskey bottle. She felt a twist in the pit of her stomach, steeled herself, wondered why she was still here. Damon had, in the beginning, captivated her with his attentions, arrested her with his hands, stunned her with his desires as he revealed to her her own longings, stopped her in her tracks by offering her a roof over her head, no questions asked; and she had stayed because she was entranced by Damon's attentions and by the

longings he stirred in her, because he sometimes made
her laugh, because he asked no questions. Late spring
slowly shed its chrysalis, summer unfolded lan-
guorously, autumn erupted one day. By then, Damon—
who had always come and gone—began to stay away
more, and he drank more heavily when he returned, was
moody, often morose. Jamie asked no questions. She
knew—as Damon, her first lover, did not—she was
waiting for something to occur that would unmistakably signify a conclusion, having already learned that
endings inevitably unfurl in their own way, in their own
time, and that if she hindered or changed or stemmed
the flow of the inevitable she might never understand
what this relationship was, could be, had been. That, she
reminded herself, was why—in part, for there were
other things too, almost as important: the season, the
fact that she was penniless—she was still here: a certain
time had not yet come, whatever would happen had not
yet happened, those longings Damon had awakened in
her were fathomless. He studied her with feigned con-
sternation, asked: Cold?

It's snowing, Damon, she replied. And freezing in here.

The stove will cut the chill.

Not by much, and not for long.

She turned back to the oven, gazed into it. Damon
walked to her, put his hands on the back of her chair,
leaned over her shoulder, touched his nose to her hair. You
smell like cheap tobacco, he said. Soot, fire. Something.

She dropped her palms onto her thighs, said nothing.

Been up at Margaret's?

Where else?

Did you see that trapper?

The freeze seeped through the floorboards, elemental, substantial. Jamie shifted forward in the chair, felt the oven's heat on her face.

Well?

Well, what?

Was the trapper there?

Galen, you mean.

Galen, I mean. At Margaret's, I mean.

No, she said.

No. But you smell like him.

And you smell like whiskey. And you've been gone three days.

Damon put his arms around her. As he always did, unrepentant after his absences, unrepentant in drink, bridging with his body the chasms that lay between one unkindness and the next. She knew without asking that he'd been with his wife.

I don't like you smelling of trapper, he told her.

She sighed. I cleaned Margaret's fireplace, she said. It was exactly what he wanted to hear.

⌐

By the time Jamie walked into the pizza parlor, she'd come three weary days' distance, much of it on foot,

toting a small army-surplus knapsack holding everything she could carry and with the dog on a leash. She'd
stayed to back-country roads that led away from the
small town she'd lived in all her life until she left it,
keeping a wary eye out for troopers, afraid of being
picked up for hitchhiking even if she were just walking
along the road, afraid of being stopped by any authority,
questioned, asked for identification, afraid of being taken
back. She wasn't truant—she'd quit school—but an
orphan, a word that in no way described the visceral blow
of burying her mother, or her grief or aloneness, a word
worse than truant, for truants were not, like orphans,
wards of the state. Jamie had no choice but to leave where
she was from, had none now but to take no chances or
she'd find herself in a foster home, without the dog—the
social worker had coldly insisted upon that, made it clear
that the dog would be taken from her and placed in an
animal shelter, and Jamie could not bear the thought of
losing the only thing she had left in the world to love, the
only creature she trusted to love her unreservedly in
return.

She saw no county sheriffs, for they were mostly
attending to rural disorders—treed cats and family
squabbles, the infrequent break-in or drive-by
shooting—and no state police, for they were mostly
patrolling the highways that had within her own
memory cut swaths through entire states, bypassing,
emptying out, city and town centers and spawning unco-

incidental suburbs and malls alongside their multilaned routes. The country roads that had once been primary routes were not now even secondary or much of anything, and few vehicles passed her. She and the dog rode twice, once for a few miles and the second time for a few hours, in the back of pickup trucks that first day; and the first night out they sheltered in a badly rundown barn that sat beside the foundation stones of a farmhouse long before burned to the ground, Jamie unaware that the bats unfurling their wings and dropping from the rafters at dusk would in a whoosh rush through the gaping roof before dawn and, distressed and disturbed by human and canine presence, wake and terrify her by flitting madly, menacingly about. The second day a traveling salesman of veterinary equipment gave them their first lift, toward afternoon's end, and dropped the two close to the state line, the second in as many days. The border was unremarkable but for a small sign indicating its existence, and Jamie's exhilaration: two days, she realized, two crossings, and now she was that much closer to the small town where her mother happened to have been born, a place that happened to be on Jamie's way by dint of circumstance, because she happened to have visited it once before. She fussed over the dog, kissed its nose after they passed the sign, stepped into that third state and went on, her sorrow deep and not diminished but somehow softened by the long, quiet going. At sunset she came upon an abandoned spate of weathered

cabins—the first of which bore the painted words, Pine
Island View—whose grounds were riotous with blos-
soming weeds, wildflowers, tender thistle, saplings, the
promise of dense briar, and whose boundaries were
indiscernible for the haphazard encroaching of new
forest growth. She and the dog slept on a porch of rotting
floorboards belonging to the cabin farthest from the
road, and in the morning she walked about, looking for
the motel's namesake, but found no island, no pines, no
pond. Nor could she say where the view might be or had
ever been.

That day she got a ride from a woman in a stationwagon who was hauling a massive cedar hopechest
somewhere. I never stop for bums, the woman told her,
but a dog's something else. The woman dropped her and
the dog at a filling station that had two dilapidated red
pumps, a service garage whose rusted doors had been
bolted shut before Jamie was born, and what must have
once been an office but now looked more like a shack,
out of which a grizzled man of indeterminable age who
considered himself familiar with incontestable misfor-
tune emerged to pump gas. Fill 'er up, the woman told
him. That, and: She ain't going my way.

He took her in with one glance before Jamie even
got close to going around the back of the station, saw
that she couldn't have been on the road for more than a
few days and that she already had the look of someone
content enough with the situation to keep on going for

a few weeks, a few months, a few years, until someone or something stopped her; and he figured she'd accept whoever that someone or whatever that something was for only so long before she hit the road again, because she also had the look of someone who had learned how easy it was to walk away from whatever it was she'd left behind and mistake that for what folks call a solution. He recognized that, and he also took in the American flag patched upside down on one cheek of her backside, saw that those jeans with their frayed bottoms were at least secondhand if not thirdhand and maybe not even patched by her. Even if they were, he reckoned, that distress signal matched in no way the gravity of the distress she held within her, obvious to him despite that square-shouldered gliding rootless walk because of the way she hadn't so much as asked to use the washroom, not because it wasn't hers to use but because she didn't want to appear to need to use it, didn't want to seem to have any needs whatsoever. And she was too young not to have any needs, he saw immediately, being younger than the law allowed for someone to be on their own, even if they did have a mutt by their side.

She wordlessly took the dog around the back and the woman drove away, and he told himself seven minutes and checked his watch, went back into the shack wondering just how many good-for-nothing bearded longhairs, draft-dodgers, dropouts (sometimes accompanied by young, brazen, braless women, always spilling

out of Beetles or beatup VW vans, always buying as little
gas as they could get away with in order to use the washroom) he'd seen in the last decade—this being, as his
sadly swollen and diabetic wife always put it, the Year of
Our Lord nineteen hundred and seventy-six, may God
bless us and may God bless America—and decided that
no matter the count, he'd seen far too many for his liking.

And in exactly seven minutes Jamie appeared in the
doorway, having washed her hands and face and tied
back her hair and, he figured, probably brushed her
teeth and wiped down the sink with a paper towel. With
the dog leashed to her and that knapsack on her back,
she asked him politely—as though he were running a
diner and not a godforsaken filling station—if he might
have something for the dog to drink from, might sell her
a cup of coffee. He leaned back, scrutinized her, folded
his hands. Asked: Are you one of them hippies?

I don't think so, she replied after a moment. I never
thought about it.

He asked where she was going, and she told him. He
asked where she'd come from, and she said: A ways. He
poured coffee from the pot on the one-eyed burner into
a chipped cup and told her to drink it outside, then
scrounged about for the pie pan he knew had to be
somewhere and eventually found it, went to the washroom and saw with the satisfaction of foreknowledge
that she'd wiped down the sink. He filled the pan with
water and came back around and set it down for the

dog. She thanked him and handed him a quarter. He turned the coin over between his fingers, examined it as though he'd never seen currency in his life, gave it back to her with a scowl. That brew's not worth a plugged nickel, he told her.

The dog had settled at her feet by the time she finished the coffee. With any luck, the man mentioned before she could thank him again as she handed him the cup, you might get to where you're going today.

Well, I'm not what anyone would call lucky, she remarked, with such neutrality, such maturity, that he, who knew better than most the sinister vagaries of always having to struggle just to call something a life that was hardly a life at all, looked hard at her in surprise, thinking that he had misread her age and realizing that he hadn't, for she looked no older and was no older than when he'd first laid eyes on her. That she had come to this conclusion—one the most unquestionably unfortunate and hapless people he knew resisted, rebuffed, rejected even as they slid from one adversity to another—caught him off guard, softened him. Hell, he admitted, it's a shame but it's a fact: luck's a rare thing. And then accepted her thanks once again and watched her make her way down the road, with that dog walking nice as anyone could please beside her, toting that knapsack on her back and holding that impenetrable and wholly private distress close within her.

Two young houseframers with wages in their

pockets and a couple of six-packs between them
stopped for her along the road late that afternoon, said
sure, they were going her way, settled her and the dog in
the back of their truck. She leaned the knapsack against
their toolboxes and then leaned against it, watched the
landscape with its few and far between rundown ham-
lets and dilapidated, empty truckstops roll past, eventually huddled down to escape the blow, dozed. When the
vehicle slowed and stopped, she awoke with a start, sat
up, saw the pizza parlor, the woods around it, the small
parking lot, the narrow road. The two framers spilled
out of the pickup's cab and, hardly able to stand, hung
on for a moment to the doors they slammed shut.
Where are we? she asked, and the driver looked up at the
sound of her voice and said, Oh shit, then doubled over
with laughter.

They stumbled into the pizza parlor, arms over each
other's shoulders. She climbed out of the truck and got
her knapsack and the dog down, undid her hair and
tried to comb it with her fingers before tying it back
again, hoisted the knapsack on and walked the dog
beyond the two cars in the lot, then stood in the road,
stared in both directions, saw no route sign, no houses,
nothing at all. The sun was swollen, low on the horizon,
and she thought to walk on and knew that she could not
without knowing which way to go. She brought the dog
back to the curb and crouched before it, asked, What do
you think?, was met by the dog's quizzical stare, a lick to

her face. I don't know, she admitted, I just don't know. And then rose and turned toward the pizza parlor, where a large woman in an apron stood before the door, arms folded. Them fools, the woman said to her. That, and: If that dog has manners, bring it on in and put it in the corner where there ain't no tables.

The framers were hunched over their drinks at the bar. Two other men at a table looked away from the television that sat on the bar's end, watched Jamie choose a seat near it, exchanged raised-eyebrow glances. She ordered a plain pizza, a coke. You don't look like you can eat a whole pizza, the aproned woman said to her, and if you're fixing to share it with that dog, you'd better do it outside.

A napkin and fork and knife appeared before her, and Jamie went to the washroom and rinsed the dust from her face, took a bill from the thin fold of ones and fives and tens she had stowed deep in a pocket, returned to her seat. The framers were gone. She sipped her coke, and when the pizza came she ate slowly, eyeing the dog from time to time. The woman served whiskey to the men at the table and came back behind the counter, leaned on her elbows. So, she asked, where you going?

Dyers Corner.

What, tonight?

Is it far?

Damon, the woman called over to the men, how far to Dyers Corner?

Jamie turned for his answer. He cocked his head to

the side, put his glass down, replied: About forty miles.

This girl needs a lift there. The dog too.

He laughed then, shook his head. The other man asked her: What's in Dyers Corner?

I don't know, she told him.

You been there before?

Once.

Then there's no reason to go again. 'Less you have folks there.

She shook her head. I figured I'd be able to get a bed for the night. Maybe for a few nights. See the reservoir.

He slugged back the whiskey, let out a long ah. First of all, the only inn Dyers Corner ever had was boarded up some years back. Second, you sure as hell don't have to go there if you just want to see the reservoir. Not that the reservoir's anything to see.

Maybe there's a motel somewhere?

Maybe not, the man scoffed. But Damon here will take you to his place. He's got an extra room for chippies.

TJ, lay off, the woman warned. Pay him no mind, she told Jamie. And go on out and give some of that to the dog. If anybody drives up, pretend you're eating it yourself.

Jamie piled slices onto the napkin and slid off the stool, went outside with the dog and made it sit, sat beside it, pulled the pizza apart, fed the creature. TJ eventually came out and grinned at her, got into a car, backed out into the waning light, drove off. She watched his taillights recede, wiped her hands as best she could on the greasy napkin, went back inside. She cornered the dog beside her knapsack again, paid the bill, left a tip, pocketed her change. If you don't mind, she said to the woman, I'll just use the washroom again. It don't matter to me, the woman replied.

Damon was at the bar, keys in hand, when Jamie returned. You might as well come along, he said, unless you want to spend the night and most of tomorrow walking to Dyers Corner. Or sleeping in the woods and walking most of tomorrow and the next day.

Go on with him, the woman said, he won't hurt you. He's a married man.

In a manner of speaking, Damon amended.

Jamie hesitated.

It's no trouble to him at all, the woman told her, and he won't bother you. Damon opened his hands, keys dangling from a finger. I'm leaving, he said, your choice. And so Jamie took her knapsack and the dog and put both in the backseat of his—borrowed, he mentioned— car, and they drove into a dusk that quickly became darkness. A while later they drove onto a causeway, and at the sight of the reservoir Jamie's breath caught in her throat. She asked him to stop—she who had said nothing to him—and Damon obliged, pulled to the side and cut the engine. She rested her forehead and the fingertips of one hand against the passenger window, looked out over the reservoir she'd last seen when eleven but had never seen under any canopy of stars; and he watched a vein pulse in her neck, studied her small hand and fine fingers, her thick hair. He was astounded by how young, how unselfconscious, how trusting she was, and found himself unsure as to how vulnerable she might be.

She sat motionless a long time, remembering that the bus had smelled of cheap perfume and coarse tobacco, recalling the tilt of the driver's cap, the blur of budding forests reddening in a late-spring sunset, the way her mother had pulled on prim white gloves over her cleaningwoman's hands and straightened her hat before they claimed their one suitcase from the bus's bay at their journey's end. They'd walked from the bus station to her grandmother's dark apartment with its yellow lightbulbs, walked to that dingy, low-slung, red-brick building erected a century before to house working people and into that apartment that hadn't had a fresh coat of paint for years. It was small and spartan and solid, nothing like the ramshackle place Jamie's mother had grown up in, where Jamie's grandmother had taken in laundry and where, her mother told Jamie, her grandfather had gone on the dole and almost lost his mind. When Jamie had asked what the dole was, her mother laughed; she remembered that, and that they'd buried her grandmother the next day, beside her grandfather, and she could still see her mother's gloved hand closing a coffin lid, her mother packing a box of keepsakes and cording it with twine for the return bus trip, the two of them eating macaroni-and-cheese at a diner with a green formica counter. The next day her mother hired a man with a car who drove them to the reservoir, and Jamie to this day retained an impression of his face, but not exactly where they were when he stopped and pulled alongside the downed fencing, and not his voice when he said: I'll wait for you here. And then she had followed her mother through a forest of dappled light, her mother breaking off branches as they went so as to find their way back, followed her through ferns already uncurling and past ghostly birches and lofty oaks, skirting the flowering dogwood, brambly blackberry bushes, poison ivy. When they reached the water it had seemed to Jamie that the reservoir shimmered and stretched on forever, and they climbed atop a granite out-crop and sat there, ate boiled eggs and apples. Jamie could not conjure any picnic basket, not even a paper bag, only her mother's words. I don't know where their place was—she could hear her mother's voice even now—but it was somewhere here, maybe in the middle. I've no idea. Your grandmother came back only once, and she didn't bring me with her. She wasn't a back-looking person, and neither am I. But I thought you should know where she was from.

Jamie had asked: Am I a back-looking person?

And her mother had answered: I'd say certainly not.

The window's glass felt cool on Jamie's forehead, the

palm of her hand, her fingers. Fireflies glittered, hovered just above the causeway's edge, multiplied of a sudden and rose thickly above the shore's spread, pinpricks of flitting light reflecting myriad in the water below the star-studded sky. She watched them in silence, recalling, remembering. And then Damon gently twisted a strand of her hair about one finger, leaned toward her, asked: Lost in space?

No, she told him. Just lost.

Two

After being untied, the boy made his way to the junkyard where he lurked among the rusted hulks of twisted
metal and for a while made himself comfortable in the
cab of a wrecked car and watched his family's comings
and goings, his eyes as colorless and expressionless as
the fishbelly sky. He thought of nothing in words and
so gave no thought to those things he saw before him,
the debris-littered yard and clapboard house and shoddy
outhouse and, beyond these, doorless and precarious
sheds that gaped darkly within and from which spewed
dented barrels and discarded pipes and discolored cor-
rugated siding and rotting beams and rolls of rusted
wire and countless other things in varying states of
decomposition. He gave no thought to the graceful
oaks that, bereft of leaves, notched their stark shapes
into the sky on the far side of the outbuildings, none to

the hanging tree—a massive denuded maple—from
which no deer carcass hung, none to the ropes that
dangled from it. He understood all things for what
they were, apparent and immediate or not so, familiar
or not so, and here all was familiar and apparent: the
clutter, the buildings, the trodden trail of spilt slop
leading to the distant pigsty far beyond the sight of the
house, the footprints frozen in the muck before the
door's muddied wooden stairs, those who came from
inside the house only to disappear into it once again. He
lurked and settled, waited and watched, and now and
then made noises in his throat for no particular reason.

At times a whiff of flaring creosote and burning
pine came his way, though the smoke from the
stovepipe tilting out of the clapboard siding blew
upward in spirals far from him. The boy hunkered
down below the opening where the car's windshield
had once been each time the door to the house opened,
and he held his breath on the way up, peering over the
edge of the stripped dashboard. Twice the mute—perhaps his cousin, perhaps an uncle, he'd not been told
and would not, anyway, have cared—pushed his way
outside and stumbled some distance from the house
and relieved himself only to stand and gape, pants
unzipped and hands dangling at his sides, at what he
had done. Both times the woman, whom the boy knew

was called Ada and who was his mother, shrieked at the
mute from somewhere inside, and both times the mute
responded in the manner of a slow-witted dancing
bear, rocking solemnly from foot to foot until she
appeared, shapeless and shortlegged, with prod in hand
to drive him indoors. The limp-gaited man who had
tied the boy to the tree, whose name was Jake and who
was the boy's father, appeared several times, once to
rummage among some hand-wringer washing machines
and discarded potbellied stoves, once to bring in wood,
once to kill a chicken. He strung the bird up by its feet
from an old swingset and wrung its neck, and before it
was dead cut off its head and stepped back unevenly
and watched its wings flap and the blood spray until it
stilled lifeless, and then the woman came out and began
to pluck it. The man tried to mount her as she did but
she belted him and he set off for the outhouse, listing
each time he stepped with that kneestraight,
unbending shorter leg, and then did not reappear until
she had taken the carcass inside and the feathers rolled
aimlessly about.

The boy had no way to track time, of which he had
nothing but anyway, and so he could not have said when
both the man and the woman came out of the house,
Ada with a pail of slops and Jake emptyhanded, and
went their separate ways. When they disappeared from

sight the boy moved fast, though once inside the house the shock of woodstove heat stopped him long enough for the mute to notice him and break into a shuffle. He threatened the idiot with Ada's prod and the mute backed himself into a wall, and then the boy went helter-skelter through the chaos, through strewn clothes and garbage, running his hands along the countertops crowded with empty bottles and springs and metal rings and filthy cans and crashing these to the floor, rifling through half-open drawers and pocketing trash as well as an old lighter and cans of lighter fluid and a sheathed blade. He grabbed a musty jacket from a hallway peg and an earflap hat too big for him by half and stuffed handfuls of rusks into a frayed fowlsack, which he tossed onto his shoulder. He passed his youngest sibling, a silent unnamed child leashed to a bedpost, but paused before the girlchild, his sister, who sat rocking herself, hand in mouth, on a broken stool in a back room. She did not look at him even when he flicked the lighter open and struck the flint, menacing her, and she could hardly have seen him through her unkempt hair if she did. He tired of the threat and flipped the lid back and slapped her hard just once, lighting out to the sound of her whimper.

He did not set off down the drive in Jake's unbal-anced footsteps but raced soundlessly, intent, down through the woods on the hillside beyond the cliff, and when he reached a stand of pines above the road he treed himself, perched high and hidden, caught his breath. His palms stung from being scraped against the bark and pitch spots were already beginning to blacken on them by the time Jake limped into view.

He threw a fit stomping around that tree where the boy should have been but was not. He left the rope where it was and circled outward and into the road and back into the brush in an ever-widening arc, cursing, bellowing, ranting. The boy followed his hobbled movements with a bobbing of his head and nothing else but for the opening and closing of his mouth, as though in silent mirth, watched Jake's breath come hard and white when he finally stopped humping about and stood in the middle of the road. His father skewed his face and narrowed his eyes and turned unevenly then, looking into the forest, and the boy went rigid and outlasted him, unseen. *Judds,* the man called out once, twice: *Juh-uhhhds.*

The boy stayed treed long after his father went off in the direction of the trailer park, where he rapped on doors and demanded with foul breath and mean temper to learn from those and their children within what had happened to his trussed son, and the boy climbed down at dusk and did nothing but sit with his back against the trunk until the dog came at him. He then scrambled to his feet and stayed very still while the creature regarded him with great interest. From somewhere came the sound of a whistle, two, and the dog looked in the direction of the sound but did not move off. After some time, the boy reached into a pocket very slowly and pulled out the knife and unsheathed it, took a cautious step toward the dog, made a swiping motion. Much to his surprise, the dog sat. The boy moaned and slashed at the air again and the dog thumped its tail and lay back its ears with a canine grin, then sprung away. The boy squatted and stared at the creature, uncomprehending, and then the dog stretched backend up, yawned, drew close. This time the boy did not raise the knife, nor did he move, and the dog nosed him, sniffed his wrists and knees and face. When the boy moaned again, the dog licked him; and then he fell back, the dog suddenly upon him in delight, the boy's nostrils filling with fur scent and sweet canine breath as he rolled about on the ground, the dog leaping over and around him, feigning nips, growling playfully, until the boy was breathless. When the dog left, he lay where he was and stared into the darkening sky through the pinetops for a long time before searching for the knife and finding and sheathing it, then making for the direction in which the dog had headed. Eventually he broke out onto the road, and at the first house he saw, hid himself beyond it. Much later, but sometime before the dog came to him in the middle of the night, he lifted his face to the snow, let the flakes melt into his eyes.

Three

The dog whined, the sound seeping in through the seams of her sleep, and Jamie struggled out from under the dream's weight and the covers she'd pulled over her head, put her socked feet on the floor and, taking one of the blankets off the bed and wrapping it around her, tiptoed through the room's dank cold. Damon slept a drunken, spent slumber, did not stir. The dog whined again, pawed at the door as she felt her way down the stairs, turned circles before she muffled the latch as best she could and let it out. She stood in the doorway like a bedraggled apparition disturbed and disturbing on the threshold of a world obscured by snowfall, into which the dog disappeared. Jamie peered into the swirling whiteness, into the blank beyond, could see nothing. She waited for the dog to return and when it did not she closed the door and, turning on no light and wrapping the blanket more tightly around her, went and sat in one of the two old armchairs by a window whose panes had frosted. She brooded, tried to clear away the webs of her nightmare—of a deer, shot through its windpipe and making a sickening, sucking noise, of her running alongside the creature through phantom birches until both reached a lake's edge, of the lake turning to marble as the deer leaped onto it, landing crazily and with legs akimbo, spraying abstract crimsoned patterns across a grayveined surface that did not give, of the boy who materialized from nowhere in the deer's bloody wake, of the lake slowly imploding, disappearing both deer and boy beneath great marble shards that floated about, settled into floes, became solid ice—and shivered despite the blanket, wrapped herself within it more tightly.

The dog barked, not to be let in but in the distance and as if in play. She listened for it to paw at the door, but it did not come, and after a while she rose, went to the threshold, opened the door once again, clapped her hands softly. Handclaps echoed back at her, distinctly, and the sound propelled her backward, the blanket dropping from her shoulders as the dog raced out of the murk, brushed by her. And then she saw the boy, running along the road's edge, slipping and sliding, and she did not know whether her heartbeat or the boy's footsteps were pounding in her ears, pulled the door hard

and fumbled with its lock and braced herself against it.
The dog beside her stood with ears straining forward.
Upstairs, Damon shifted, turned in his sleep, the bed
creaking; and she held her breath, hoping against hope
that he might wake, but he did not. The dog eventually
settled down, lay on the floor. When Jamie's terror
finally subsided, she stooped, retrieved the blanket,
made her way to the armchair and made a cocoon of the
cover, curled into it. And then slept fitfully, afraid to
dream, afraid to wake.

∽

The snow accumulation, tamped down by the
midday sun's meager warmth, by afternoon froze with a
glazed bluish crust as the temperature plummeted.
Damon woke and sobered, listened to country music on
the radio, went out once to tap on the gas cylinder on
the side of the house but could not tell how far from
empty it was, set the faucet taps to dripping so the pipes
would not freeze, lifted the receiver of the telephone that
had been disconnected for months and listened to the
dead line, played solitaire. He said little; he always said
little after drinking hard, and he often drank hard in
order to dampen, trample, the remorse and resentment
and confusion he was unable to keep at bay except with a
bottle, since he was nagged by the unbearable realization

that his best years were behind him. They had passed without Damon even knowing they were his best—those teenage years of beer-guzzling, rum-and-coke parties, of Thursday night and Saturday afternoon football games with him sitting in uniform on the bench as a second-stringer, of the countless evenings he'd borrowed his old man's car and gone necking with the high-school sweetheart he married as soon as he got back from the service—because he could never have imagined that after those years things beyond his control, things he didn't understand, would pull the rug from underneath him and leave him jobless and downward-spiraling, his benefits finished (he hadn't wanted to apply for them, having been taught and believing even now although he knew otherwise that anyone on unemployment was a slacker, but he'd relented, applied for unemployment anyway, swallowing his pride and his humiliation), his wife back in town and on her own, not blaming him but on her own and working, waiting, she said, for him to figure things out. Except the only thing he could figure out was that the rent on this place was unpaid and that there was no money for food, never mind heating oil. And no matter the girl, whose youth and perfectly flawless skin and yielding ways had made him feel (along with the whiskey) as though he were once again back in high school, reckless and predatory, he was on the verge of having to face the fact that the past was past and that his wife, uncomplainingly working hard to make a life for both of them, was now—to complicate matters—pregnant.

Jamie left him alone. She stomped a narrow path from the door to the road in a pair of ill-fitting work-boots not originally her own, wandered the road and then the woods behind the house with the dog, thinking she might find some trace of the boy and not knowing what she would do if she did. There was no sign of him. When she returned to the house she found Damon where she'd left him, at the table silently shuffling cards. She said nothing and did not take off her jacket, went upstairs to dust and sweep, to scrub down the bathroom, to mop, then went back downstairs and did the same, moving about to stay warm. Damon had not put on the oven. When TJ arrived Damon did not break out the whiskey but sat with him at the kitchen table, their heads bent conspiratorially and their voices low, and Jamie went back outside with the dog, walked toward the trailer park, to the tree where the boy had been tied, saw that the plow had banked snow on that side of the road and that there were no footprints about the tree. She got back to Damon's just as TJ was leaving. Nice and cozy in there, TJ meanly remarked as he passed her in the yard.

Jamie did not wonder how long Damon would stay; she knew it was only a matter of time, a matter of whiskey, a matter of satiation (though she barely understood this), and she asked nothing, said nothing to him when she entered the house. She pulled a chair over to the stove, turned on the oven, sat before it. Damon eventually went upstairs and returned with the whiskey bottle and poured himself a drink, another, waited for the liquor to loosen his tongue. When it did, he told Jamie in an offhand way that TJ might have an interior painting job lined up for them, then drank the more to soften his remorse, regret, confusion at not being able to admit that it was over between them. He drank until he became effusive, deceitfully considerate, finally insisting that he fry the last of the bacon and eggs for dinner and serve her. Jamie ate slowly, still wearing her jacket, eyeing the can of bacon drippings on the counter, knowing there would be nothing left to eat—and no more whiskey—in a few days. Then let herself be swept away.

Four

At The Four Corners, whose lone store in her grandparents' time had years before given way to a huddle of
improbable buildings—a convenience store, a filling station, a quonset hut the size of a small stable that Jamie
knew no purpose for, a one-room brick post office with
an aluminum-and-glass door—she found her post office
box empty, Margaret's check unaccountably still not
there. She was almost out the door when the postmaster
appeared behind the counter and said: Jamie Hall.

She let go of the handle and turned as the door
closed, a gush of frigid air at her back. Do you have mail
for me?

He motioned to her, his head with its few strands of
long white hair wobbling, rummaged below the counter
that cut him off waisthigh. He lost his breath with the
effort of bending, caught it as he straightened, held up

in an unsteady hand a soiled envelope with her name and nothing else written on it. It's not right, he told her when she reached him. Not even a stamp.

I'm sorry.

Pain flowed into his shoulder, down an arm. His hand fluttering.

You can stamp it, she ventured, fingering a pocket for the little change she had.

Never mind. It has no address anyway. You can't send a proper letter without an address.

It's probably not a letter.

Well, it's in an envelope.

She waited. The postmaster placed it on the counter, his hands and wrists translucent but for the mottling and blue veins and opaque yellow nails. He leaned on his elbows to lessen the tremors. Thank you, she said, leaving the envelope between them.

He considered her. Well, he responded, it doesn't much matter. It doesn't happen too often.

No.

You look just like your grandmother.

You always say that.

Yes, I do. I was very taken with her, will never forget her. And I was close behind her that last day, the day we left our homes, the valley, everything we had. I saw her leave your grandfather's side, watched her sit down at some distance from us, sorrowful, despairing, weeping like there was no tomorrow. Grieving. Purely grieving.

His expression went vacant and Jamie did not reach for the envelope. He was lost to all she could never fully know, as he'd been among those who once peopled the valley and retreated before the waters rose to eradicate all traces of their existence, submerging their lives until that time under a liquid darkness that in the end became—for him, for her family—a treacherous, predatory clement. Jamie had discovered, in her wanderings at the reservoir's edge in futile search of a granite outcrop, that she too instinctively, intensely distrusted the water, feared it, as if this distrust and fear had been willed to her through blood. *Come*, Damon once beckoned to her on a hot summer afternoon as he slipped into the reservoir's shallows, but she was unnerved by what she imagined lay beneath the water and would not go. She'd watched him swim away, her heart full in her throat, and when the dog worried a snake at the lake's edge her sense of foreboding was given an ominous specificity.

The postman blinked severally, said as if reading her thoughts: Some people swim in the reservoir, although it's forbidden.

I know.

I wouldn't myself. There are graves, after all. The

dead were left behind. But I worked for some winters cutting ice, and I had no reservations about walking out onto that lake despite the fact that it never freezes over entirely. Most others from the valley would have no truck with it, no matter the season. Your grandmother, for one. She always said water was a mighty changeable thing, but water nonetheless.

She was right.

You know, he continued, the reservoir once receded after many years of drought, so that what was left of the houses reappeared. Some of the people who had left their homes came back then, one August Sunday, just to look, and your grandparents were among them. Some of us had skiffs, and I persuaded your grandmother to allow me to row her out—your grandfather wanted nothing to do with it—and we floated between the homes, just below the attics. I remember the way your grandmother held on to the sides of the boat, so hard that her knuckles were white. I remember that, and the silence.

She watched his eyes cloud, his jaw work, wondered how old he might be. He once told her that he'd outlived everyone, including her grandmother, whose countenance, he had added, lived on in Jamie.

He sighed, pushed the envelope toward her. At my age there's little else but the past, he said.

She touched the back of his hand, said goodbye. She

opened the envelope in the convenience store. The piece of paper inside bore no greeting or signature, and only two words: *Deer meat.* She placed the message back into the envelope and folded it into a jacket pocket. The smell of coffee wafted strongly, made her mouth water. The pockfaced cashier watched her hawkishly, tongued her gums, and Jamie moved beyond the woman's stare, wandered the cramped aisles. One customer, two, came and went, the cashier punching numbers, the register ringing, its drawer clanking open, being slammed shut. When Jamie made her way back to the front of the store, she had nothing in hand. The cashier crossed her arms and sucked at her teeth, pushed her tongue into a cheek, distorted her moonscape face.

I wonder if I could buy a few things on credit, Jamie said.

The cashier grunted.

Excuse me?

You don't have credit here.

Well, Jamie told her reasonably, I thought maybe I could.

I don't know what gave you that idea, the cashier replied, then rolled her tongue into a cheek again.

You know me, Jamie said, not insisting, still reasonably, you know I cash my checks here, the ones from Margaret Horan—

Cashing checks is one thing, credit's another, the cashier interrupted, narrowing her eyes, uncrossing her arms, placing her hands on the counter. The backs of her hands were strangely smooth. Store policy, she added.

Jamie hesitated, fingered the change in her pocket, said: Thanks anyway. The cashier picked at her skin above an eyebrow, pursed her mouth, looked off. When Jamie stepped out of the store, the postmaster was standing in the post office doorway, and he watched her neither stride nor walk but just glide, her way of moving exactly that of her grandmother, across the lot—empty but for his ancient DeSoto—between the convenience store and the filling station, her hair glossing in the winter light and her chin held at a slight tilt, her breath curling white, the bleach of light reflecting off the snow diminishing her already extraordinary thinness. He pushed open the door to better see, but his eyes rheumed because of the frigid air and his vision blurred, so that she became much like his memory, inexact, ephemeral. He rubbed at his eyes, dug his knuckles into them. By the time he could see clearly, she was nowhere in sight.

↫

Jamie walked the last mile numbly, the reservoir receding behind her and the world hushed but for the fall of her footsteps. She did not alter her pace but now and then stumbled, the lack of feeling in her feet oddly painful, the soles of the boots crunching hard. When the dog scented her a stretch from the house, it raced toward her, greeted her wildly, cavorted about as it accompanied her to the door. Inside, she saw the drained whiskey bottle on the table, heard Damon move around overhead, knew by the way he came down on his heels that he was getting ready to leave. She dragged a chair over to the stove, sat, turned on the flame, pulled off her boots, cradled one foot then the other in her hands, rubbed each in turn. The oven began to give off a rancid, hot-metal smell, and the kitchen faucet dripped with the cadence of a muffled metronome.

She did not turn her head as Damon came down the stairs. He smelled of cologne. He went to the sink and turned the faucet hard, allowed the water to gush, slowed it to a trickle once again. He hated the hopeless situation, his infinite cowardice, raged inwardly because of both and because of the junkman's appearance in Jamie's absence.

The well will go dry if we run it all winter, she said.

Where were you? he demanded.

It was past noon, Damon. You were still asleep.

That's not what I asked.

The post office: I went to the post office.

Did Margaret's check come?

It wasn't there. Maybe next week.

Maybe next week, he mimicked. Well, maybe next week's too late. Too late, he repeated, then said: And, by the way, the junkman was here.

Jamie glanced quizzically at Damon then. The junkman?

Looking for his boy.

His boy?

Yeah, looking for his boy. He thought you might know something. Said he'd tied him to a tree near the bus stop some days back, that someone untied him. A girl with a dog. Some bitch with a mutt, was how he put it.

She stared into the oven, said nothing.

So? Damon asked.

I didn't know who he was, she replied after a moment.

Well, that was him. And I don't like it: I don't like the junkman, and I don't like the junkman coming around here looking for you.

For me? Or the boy?

I'd say for you. For interfering.

That's not what I'd say.

Oh?

What, she asked with a sigh, would you have done? Left him there?

I would've thought twice before butting into other

people's business.

If I thought twice, she said slowly, looking over at Damon, looking at him squarely, I'd think it was wrong to tie someone to a tree.

Well, as a matter of fact, the boy's not right in his head.

He was tied like an animal.

Good of you to tell me.

Damon, there's no reason—

There's no reason for you to put your nose where it doesn't belong.

There's no reason to argue. Except if you're looking for an excuse to storm out of here, when you're going anyway.

I don't need any excuse. Seeing there's nothing to stay for.

She swallowed hard, faced the oven again. Meaning the whiskey's finished, she said.

That too.

TJ's car slowed before the house, braked, idled. Damon crossed the room. There was, Jamie knew, no stopping him.

Damon, she said evenly, I can't do this much longer.

Don't, he told her, then was gone. When the dog came over and licked her hands, she buried her face in its fur. Much later, she opened a can of dog food, stared at the contents hungrily, put it into a bowl and placed it on the floor, then boiled water with a few spoonfuls of sugar, drank a cup of that, part of a second. She slept in an armchair, fully dressed and wrapped in blankets, with the oven off. Mice scampered in the walls, and to their patter Jamie dreamed the boy tapping at the window. When she rose before dawn, the last of the sugar water was frozen in the cup she'd placed on the floor beside her.

↜

She waited past Christmas—her first alone, a day she tried to convince herself was like any other although it wasn't—for Damon to return, but he did not. She became unsure whether he would. The cold became pernicious. When all the food but some flour was gone, she made a dough with what little was left, fried bread in the last of the bacon fat, the grease coagulating as the patties cooled and the bread tasting oddly sour. She ate by the oven, and after nightfall the gas gave out. Jamie took her knapsack from a closet then, rummaged through her meager possessions, chose what to take, found a five-dollar bill in a shirt she'd discarded, folded and pocketed the money. She refused herself keepsakes, and on the bureau placed a neckerchief Damon once lent her, a piece of end-of-day glass they'd found together at the reservoir's edge, a braided leather bracelet he'd given her. When she finished packing, she handled Damon's shoehorn, his cologne, put them back where he'd placed them. She thought of leaving a note, decided against it, refused to think of him in an untoward way and told herself not to think of him at all except as someone who had simply, and without explanation, walked out of her life. If that was what he'd done.

He never promised her otherwise.

At dawn she packed the few cans of dog food she had, pulled on two sweaters and her thin jacket, hoisted the knapsack onto her shoulders, opened the door and stepped into a world trapped in ominous light. The dog trotted before her as a pickup truck drove past, poacher spotlights mounted where its sideview mirrors should have been, its tailgate down, the huge buck's antlered head hanging dulleyed and limp and bobbing lifelessly as the truck disappeared down the road. The sight of it struck Jamie as cautionary, and she decided not to take the road to Margaret's, but to cut through the woods instead. She did not lock the door behind her.

Five

The boy knew nothing of distance, not how to measure it nor its meaning, and he followed her and the dog beyond human earshot and, unbeknownst to him, downwind, and so trudged undetected through the forest in their wake, following in her footsteps a path long since narrowed by holly and dogwood that had at one time been cleared to the width of a lane by lumberjacks whose workhorses tramped it in heavy harnesses, dragging from the mountains logs with which other men built those homes and barns, sheds and fences that were now deep under the reservoir. The boy knew nothing about the woods or the mountains and he did not care, for he was neither moved by the beauty of the winter-stripped birch and oak and maple or the snowdusted stands of emerald-hued hemlock and dull-blue spruce nor bothered by difficult upward pitches nor relieved by gentle contours.

From time to time, without pausing, he pushed the earflap hat from his forehead and eyes, tugged at the fowlsack he carried, looked skyward and opened his mouth as though emitting a silent howl. He was tireless.

The logging trail she and the dog followed petered out at a waterfall, its sound muffled by the cascade of thin ice that sheathed it. The boy hung back, watched the dog stand belly-deep in a downstream pool, lap at the water, then scramble out of the stream and bound up the oppo-site bank she'd already scaled, race to where she was making her way slowly along the top of an icy ridge. When the boy stepped into the stream, its frigidity sent a shock through him but did not stop him from leaning over and, bringing his face to the water, lapping.

He kept himself hidden from her after she broke out of the forest, stepped into a plowed lane that ended at a sumac-lined wall, made her way up an unplowed drive— kicking at the snow, sometimes tossing a piece she'd loos-ened for the dog to chase—toward a lone house. The boy ducked instinctively, stayed down, crept hidden behind the stone wall and followed it around the orchard's periphery, and when he finally stopped crawling he knelt in the snow, peered over the wall's top. The orchard lay before him, and she had disappeared. The boy yipped, yipped again, and, watching the dog bound toward him, forgot her as though she had never been.

Six

Margaret's house was as Jamie last left it on the afternoon of the season's first snow, except for the frosted
slab of deer meat hanging by a hook from the wisteria.
She dropped her knapsack inside the door, turned the
thermostat to sixty, listened for the hum that came faint
and waited for the radiators to begin gurgling before
opening the interior shutters and going into the cellar to
bring up armfuls of wood, which she stacked to one side
of the fireplace. When she finished, she removed a worn
throw from an armchair and wrapped it about her,
whistled for the dog as she left the house, and headed in
the direction Galen always took when he left. She and
the dog followed the stream to where surface trickle
patterned outward in frozen ribbons and ice formed in
fantastically wrought shapes where the water bubbled
up through the earth's thin crust. The dog went on

before her, turned left onto a contour trail that traversed the mountainside just above the stream's source, led the way along the path they'd often walked during the autumn. They passed an improbable shack in the middle of nowhere, with trees poking through the beams of its caved-in roof, eventually came to a sinkhole of unfathomable depth around which Jamie had once seen timber rattlers basking slothfully under a warm September sun. There were no rattlers now, and the sinkhole's watery surface was solid with snowstreaks and midnight-hued ice. They went on, the dog still leading but slower now, paused at a series of serrated ledges that betrayed no sign of having ever been quarried despite the intertwining crescents, circles, and crisscrosses most curiously carved in vertical patterns here and there on the rock, by whom and when and why no one could say. Jamie and the dog went on until they reached a great tree felled by lightning, and there she snapped off dead, dry branches by kicking at them and hand-breaking them into kindling that she placed into the throw, which she knotted about one shoulder and filled at her hip until she could carry no more, then retraced her steps. The dog now following, lagging behind.

By the time they reached the pumphouse, ominous bruise-tinted thunderheads so blotted out the light that

the woods beyond Margaret's farthest fields formed a
solid ridge of darkness. The dog settled on the porch as
Jamie brought the kindling into the house. She closed
the door behind her, dropped the bundle near the
hearth, took off her boots and jacket. She drew the shutters and switched on a lamp, ran her hand along the
well-waxed surface of the long, narrow sidetable that
held a dull copper pot filled with dried roses of a color
that was now indeterminate. Above the table Margaret's
black-and-white photographs filled the wall, starkly
revealed splices of the world as it had once been, the
world through which Jamie's people and many others
had passed, and she straightened a photograph here,
another there. Children in suspenders and handstitched
clothes stared back at her with unchanging expressions;
cracked mudflats remained forever parched; in floodwa-
ters a house drowned solitary as a chair floated by; loggers cut deep into a tree not quite felled, and a dead
horse lay in tangled traces before a wagon; women
beneath flowered hats looked frank, their mouths
smeared dark with lipstick; a man set decoys as his dog
sat before a sunrise that sent rays streaking through the
photographer's plate. Jamie knew neither the names of
those who looked into or away from Margaret's camera
nor the words Margaret had spoken to them to elicit
from some their stares and from others their smiles and

from others their disregard; nor did she know the specificity of places, from which vantage-point Margaret had
photographed the causeway's earth-and-stone con-
struction or a torn screendoor or the flowery embroi-
dery on a skirt's hem. Each photograph was unusually
captioned in Margaret's careful script—*First Saturday,
March, 1937*, for instance, or *Summer, Wednesday, 1959*,
a series simply titled *Fridays*. Though the photographs
chronicled more than half a century, over which time
flowed endlessly, Jamie could not shake her conviction
that this glance, that rawknuckled hand, those waters,
that drought, this muddied child existed only in
(indeed, only for) that one split second in which Margaret captured them.

I can't imagine their lives before or after, Jamie once
mentioned to Margaret.

And Margaret had laughed at that, told her: This
wall of photographs is nothing but a dusting of the past
gathering dust. Sweep away the cobwebs, and what's left
is useless.

Not that Margaret dismissed the past, and not that
she would have freed herself of it or even wanted to,
knowing that the past meant memory and that anyone
without was no one at all. I've had a life of contem-
plating tragedy, which is not to say a tragic life, Margaret
once remarked, but that's not to say either that I

wouldn't do it all over again or that I wouldn't change things. It was late June, and they were sitting out the end of a breathless afternoon, the humidity and heat palpably pressing down, Galen leaning into his elbows on his knees and smoking a hand-rolled cigarette, his back half-turned to Jamie as though he were studying the mountains, as though he were unaware of, unaffected by, her presence, Margaret staring out over the day's density into the orchard wherein she'd buried one young grandchild and telling Jamie and Galen she no longer knew exactly where, as she'd left the grave unmarked and after untold years the unpruned trees so closely resembled one another and the untilled ground was so uneven it was impossible for her to say the child's resting place is here, or here, or there. Her only other grandchild was dead too, killed in the Mekong delta three years ago, his remains returned in a closed casket— could have been anyone, Margaret had mused aloud, I never opened it—and her son, the father of both, had been a suicide. A terrible thing to outlive your child, she added then, her voice even and her aged face inscrutable, especially when you can't imagine his last thoughts; but neither Jamie nor Galen knew whether Margaret meant the loss of her son or her son's loss of his. They knew only that Margaret had not buried her war-dead grandson in the orchard, though she'd burned the flag

that had been draped over her grandson's casket and
given to her, burned it in bitterness and to ashes somewhere near his brother's never-to-be-found-again grave.
He wouldn't have approved, Margaret admitted. But,
she added, the good thing as well as the bad thing about
the dead is that they're dead, so from them there's no
judgment.

And Margaret and Galen had both felt it, the small
shockwave that passed through her, heard the way
Jamie's breathing caught. Galen had glanced at Margaret
as she appraised Jamie with those quick intelligent eyes,
sensing in that quick incisive way of hers and only for a
fleeting moment that she'd touched a raw nerve, finally
penetrated what Galen thought to be the girl's imper-
turbable detachment and called her matter-of-factness,
the moment fleeting because Jamie brushed at it as she
would at a fly, rearranged herself, recovered, betrayed
nothing, asked: Judgment?

And then Galen shook his head ever so slightly as
Margaret chortled. The next time Jamie helped Margaret clean the house, she discovered a photograph she
had never seen—framed and on the wall, framed and to
be dusted—of a flag-draped coffin smalled by the
immensity of a military cemetery whose stark identical
tombstones stretched to infinity. The caption bore no
date, read simply: *Judgment.*

Jamie now ran a finger along the top of that frame, pressed the dry down of what dust there was between her finger and thumb, turned away from death and her knowledge of there being nothing at all good in it, sat down in an armchair and remained immobile, tried to think of nothing. When she finally stirred, she tiredly gathered her knapsack, went from room to room switching on lamps and leaving behind iridescent glow-pools, wandered about like one dispossessed in a world of another's making. Each step creaked a betrayal of the stairwell's dry years when she ascended the stairs, and she found the sound unnerving simply because there was no other. She stole through the upstairs foyer, felt her way into the smallest bedroom, switched on its light, unpacked her clothes. The faded blue ribbon hanging from the castiron bedframe was the room's only decoration except for an ancient vase atop a child's bureau, and the room's sparseness suited her, there being nothing she might disturb and little to remind her of everything that was not hers. When she finished putting her things into the bureau's drawers, she went into the bathroom and, avoiding her mirrored reflection, ran a hot bath, stripped and stood vulnerable before lowering herself into the water, knew an unease she had never felt within this house before. For she was disconcerted by a pervasive sense of the unfamiliar—the porcelain's smoothness, the bath's depth, the scent of Margaret's soaps and shampoo, the thickness of the towels she herself had laundered and dried and hung in perfect placement.

This is not, Jamie told herself, *trespass.* And knowing otherwise.

The storm broke after she had climbed back into her clothes and as she was cleaning the bathroom mechanically, thoroughly, in some futile attempt to regain—in her own eyes—her status as housekeeper. When she went downstairs to let the dog in, she felt its weight against the door as she opened it; and then they stood together, inside the threshold, and watched—Jamie, in astonishment—lightning streak through the wintry sky as snow spilled from above. From somewhere far beyond and below the orchard a thick strand of smoke flumed, spread, and the air began to smell sodden, burned, so that Jamie wondered whether a lightning bolt had hit, ignited, something. The snow heavied, the thunder and lightning struck almost simultaneously as the storm raged; and at one point the dog trembled, backed into the house. Jamie followed, extinguished all lights but one, sat on the braided rug and called the dog over to her, put her arms about it. She held the dog fast, thinking the while that her first memory—of being too small to reach a doorhandle, of her father opening the door—had taken shape in, was born of, such a storm.

She could not recall her father's face. She had the impression that she would know him nonetheless, recognize him effortlessly if she were to see him somewhere, anywhere, no matter the years that had passed since his disappearance; she believed that even if she were blind she'd know him, be aware if he were near. For his presence was indelibly imprinted on her, within her, a part of her—and that is all he was in her memory, a larger-than-life presence sitting across from her at a table between two windows through which they watched lightning streak crazily in a darkness not solid but cracked—a presence with an unmistakable voice saying to her: There's nothing to be afraid of, see. See, there's nothing to be afraid of.

But she saw and was afraid, witnessed the storm and was frightened, and became as outraged as only a terrified child can become. And then spoke her first word, or the first word she remembers thinking, saying, blurting: *Liar.*

Liar: the only word Jamie recalled ever saying to her father, just as her only memory of him is his presence during a storm. After that, he was no more. Jamie released the dog, stroked it, thought of how her mother had refused to leave that apartment, how she and her mother had remained, living in those rooms, eating at that table, staring out those two windows that overlooked a narrow, long useless and long unused canal that barely flowed, which in summer was thick with scum, floating garbage, the bellied-up carcasses of small animals no one could recognize from the bloat, and even when frozen in winter emanated a stench of stagnant water and death. They lived there, in that apartment, harmoniously, until her mother went into the hospital, leaving Jamie alone until she could stay there no longer, until she walked away from the doctors' failings, away from her mother's irremediable goneness, away from the long shadow of her father's absence.

Your father never said he wouldn't be back, Jamie's mother always told her. The unsaid being worse than a lie Jamie discovered, at the age of twelve, by prodding the ancient neighbor who used to babysit her to tell what she remembered of Jamie's father. He took all our money, Jamie screamed at her mother that night, so don't ever tell me again what he did or didn't say: he's *never* coming back.

And her mother had cried, Jamie glaring at her the while, furious, already remorseful: she had never seen her mother cry before. When her mother finally composed herself, dabbed away the last of her tears, she took a seat at that table between those two windows and looked out over the canal for a very long time before telling Jamie: You're old enough to think what you want. Think what you will.

Well, what do *you* think? Jamie shot back.

Your father didn't say he was going anywhere, her mother had replied slowly, and he didn't say he wasn't coming back. As far as I'm concerned, he's a missing person, which means he's simply among the missing.

Jamie buried her face in the dog's fur at the memory, groaned, listened to the storm rage overhead, pulled away and looked into those amber eyes, thinking: *Me too. I'm like him now. I'm among the missing.* The dog laid its ears back and wagged its tail, licked her nose, settled onto its side and stretched its legs out straight, sighed. Jamie did not seek out a bed or make a fire, eventually lay beside the dog and fell into an exhausted sleep. In the middle of the night the creature rose and padded through the house, then returned to curl by her side.

Seven

Time had no presence and the boy passed through it in the same way it passed him by, unmarked. He did not know the names of the days or of any number above one, and so he was unaware of the day on which he had first trailed her and the dog to the house beyond the sumac-lined wall or of how frequently he had walked through the frozen marshland or along the reservoir's icebound shore or of how many nights he had bedded in the pigsty's shed, heedless of the disgruntled and barren sow he pelted and chased into the dark and which returned with agitated constancy to the threshold, sensing in him an evil she would not engage. He felt neither joy nor trepidation at the world he encountered nor ascribed to it any significance, expanded the edges of all that became familiar and was unreflective about what remained unfamiliar, prowled with the insistence of a voyeur and the instinct of the unfettered.

The boy lingered near the sty, watched the sow undetected and at a distance as it snuffed and rooted about its slops, gobbling the mess, blowing menacingly at the unkempt girl squatting in the frozen muck some yards from it, one hand crammed into her mouth, as Ada walked slowly around, large stick in hand. His sister did not move from where she crouched, and when the woman stopped and raised her eyes to look about, the boy followed her with his expressionless gaze as she turned and surveyed all she saw, the dense, darkening woods, a false night spawned by the impending tempest, the girl soiling upon the ground and the sow moving in on her, squealing fiercely, the child and sow locking in a tangle of violent commotion that ended as suddenly as it began, the sow trotting over to the child's shit and wolfing it down, the crumpled child nearby and unmoving. The sow's sides heaved and its eyes flickered red, and when the woman started toward the girl the sow charged the broken heap in a bloodcrazed way and dragged the child beneath its belly as Ada raced beside the two and rained blows upon the sow's back until it screamed and cavorted, bucked into the air with a twist and freed itself of its drag and ran great circles around the sty until it raced into a far corner and stayed, panting and heaving, with its backend to the rails.

The woman stood over the girl for a long time without prodding her with so much as a foot or the stick. When she rolled the child over, the girl made no sound and came to rest upon an arm that should not have folded so beneath her. Then the woman lifted the girl, carried her limp form into the shed. When Ada came out, she pushed an empty barrel before her with which she blocked the threshold, and she went at the sow in a demented run, her squat body rocking from side to side and the sow too quick for her. The boy opened and closed his mouth at the sight and did so even after she abandoned the chase at the first boom of thunder, hurriedly gathered up the slops pail, made her way out of the sty, started back toward the clapboard house from where she'd come. When Ada was finally out of sight, the boy made his move and raced across the pen, vaulted the barrel, tumbled into the shed.

Shapes took form slowly in the inner dark as the storm rumbled overhead. The boy waited until he could make out the barrels, the pitchfork leaning prong-side up in a corner, the rotten wire-wrapped hay bales reeking of mold, the pile of woodshavings banked like a dune on which the girl was propped. He rummaged for the lighter and came up with it and flicked it open, struck the flint, went to the girl and waved it at arm's length before her eyes, then closed in on her and singed her hair. He wrinkled his nose at the smell, and when she did not move he burned away half of it, watched the skin of her scalp bubble, then kicked her in her chest. Blood covered her mouth, her chin. She did not move, made no sound.

Lightning and thunder brought the boy to the shed door, where he watched the sky and pulled at the flaps of his hat so they might lie flat against his ears and after some time pushed them back into wings, molded them outward with a clown's flourish. He leered at the heavens until a bolt of lightning stuck so close that he flinched, beheld zigzags in varying shades of molten metal, backed into the shed and moaned, covered his eyes until he saw nothing, then took his hands from his face and waited until he could once again see within the shed's dim interior. And then he took to breaking apart the bales of hay, scattering the fodder over the girl's legs until he could barely make out their shape, and when he finished he took the pitchfork and pierced the hay until he stuck flesh, leaned his weight into it, let it go and left it where it stood, erect as any flagless standard. He dropped the fowlsack, groped for a can of lighter fluid, pried off its cap with the knife, took a sharp whiff and staggered. He wiped at his stinging eyes with a wrist until they stopped smarting, then shouldered the fowlsack and squirted the hay until the can was empty.

There was an explosive whoosh when he set fire to the hay. Outside, the sow bellowed as the boy rushed away from the flames, tripped and fell, picked himself up and kicked at the barrel blocking his way, dislodged it. He looked back once, saw the conflagration encasing the girl, her face flaring and blackening, her eyes widening as skin melted and burned, saw her sitting like a broken doll as he watched, uncomprehending. His pale eyes reflecting white fire.

Eight

The overcast skies remained unbroken, and the snow swaddling the earth held all in keep but for the spread-winged hawks that circled lazily beneath the cloudcover and peered down with lidded eyes at the orchard's trundled, motionless surface disturbed by nothing but the dog and, beyond that and without Jamie's knowing, the boy. She had not slept well again, and her waking hours were troubled too; as she swept at the snow—which each night had blown back onto the porch despite both nights' stillness—she tried to brush away, smooth over with methodical strokes, the turbulence within her, once in a while pausing to watch the hawks lazily circling and to wonder at the deceitful calm that had descended.

Margaret seemed present in the house, standing just behind her, flitting by doorways, shadowing corners, and Jamie was unnerved to find herself wanting to speak aloud, to ask what was to be done next or to say there was little to do: the floors were mopped and waxed, the furniture polished, the kitchen and bathroom spotless, the bedding aired, rugs beaten, the framed photographs dusted, mirrors washed. Twice in the last two days Jamie had trekked along the stream and, upon returning and passing the pumphouse, expected to hear Margaret call out to her and the dog as she had that first time in late May, *Wooo-oooo, wooo-oooo, I could use a hand here, do you mind?*, she joining Margaret on her porch then and Margaret making a fuss over the dog, telling Jamie how delighted she was to find any soul emerging from the woods, for Margaret had decided on the spur of the moment to arrive several days before planned and Galen—whom Jamie did not know, as she knew no one but Damon and TJ—surely hadn't yet received Margaret's letter asking him to come on a certain date and help her open the house, rearrange furniture, push back into place what was against the walls, turn over mattresses, clear the cobwebs. And so Jamie lent a hand, glad for the toil and the companionship as they removed dustcovers and throws, pushed furniture around, took out rugs and beat them, aired mattresses, dusted and swept, mopped. At one point Margaret asked her where she was from, what she did, and Jamie answered: Near The Bend. Mostly I walk around.

Margaret straightened from rummaging through a trunk, looked at Jamie quizzically, her quick intelligent eyes assessing, put her hands on her hips for a moment. Well, she said then, maybe I could make do with some help, if you're interested.

They never told each other their ages, but it was apparent to both that there were many decades between them, between them too their disparate lives, one fully lived and the other hardly begun. Margaret tried to bridge these, but she spoke of private schools and farflung travels and doting parents—bohemian, Margaret once told Jamie, I sat at Tagore's feet, no wonder I broke the mold and married a military man, what an ass even if he did have something of Gary Cooper's vacuous good looks—and of her divorce and of her affairs and of her great love for a married man who had rediscovered the lost wax process in casting jewelry—he's now gone, Margaret had sighed—and of photography, of her passion for Marlowe and Donne and Hardy and Conrad and the history of cartography. Jamie told Margaret almost nothing, said little: she had never heard of Tagore or Marlowe, Donne, Hardy, Conrad, cartography, she did not know what it was to have been born into wealth, and she did not understand what being wealthy meant. The only people Jamie had ever known with money had just enough to pay their bills on time and in full, but even they had had to penny-pinch in order to qualify for automatic heating-oil deliveries. Which is to say that, until she met Margaret, Jamie never thought that money made much of a difference in the way people lived or spoke or thought or acted.

To her surprise, she was wrong.

Margaret was patient. She revealed her past, expecting the while that Jamie might eventually not only evince curiosity but also—Margaret was certain—ultimately let her guard down, shed those layers she'd wrapped about her soul, make an attempt to cross that great divide that separated them, disclose herself the only way Jamie could, by speaking of her own life. Which, as Margaret told Galen, was the only thing Jamie could possibly grasp at her age, not that Margaret even knew her age. But Jamie did not, would not, talk about herself, beyond admitting her likes and dislikes when pressed—the color blue (not red), hot coffee (not iced tea) even in summer, walking about (but not swimming in) the reservoir. And what Galen—who sometimes arrived with vegetables from his garden or freshly caught brook trout neatly packed between layers of sweetsmelling grasses in a wicker fishing basket, who often worked for Margaret and always refused payment in either cash or kind, and who was always so slow to address and so reluctant to look at Jamie that Jamie found it shocking that he was astonishingly quick to laugh, astonishingly at ease with Margaret, hardly shy despite the fact that he held himself aloof from Jamie— knew about Jamie, he kept to himself. Galen did not tell Margaret that Damon had taken Jamie in and that whatever rift there was between Damon and his wife, who as everyone in Dyers Corner knew was working and living in town while Damon, despite their separation, ping-ponged back and forth between her place and The Bend, could not have narrowed for the fact.

So, what is it you'd like to be? Margaret once asked Jamie in Galen's presence. And Jamie replied, not hesitating and with perfect equanimity, guarding everything within her, that she hadn't given much thought to the question and that for the moment she was just—that *just*, Margaret repeated in exasperation later to Galen— practicing, maybe even learning, to be somebody who takes each day as it comes.

Aside from that, Margaret insisted.

Aside from that, Jamie echoed, again with equanimity, I'd consider anything you suggested.

Well, Margaret told her in all seriousness, you've the build and the hands of an equestrian. Jamie, nonplussed, looked at her hands as Margaret rose, went inside to prepare tea, until she realized that Galen was watching her. Jamie looked at him then—for the first time squarely and somewhat abashedly, for she knew that he knew she didn't know the word—and he said, very quietly, Equestrian means horseback rider.

Right, Jamie rejoined. And Galen suppressed a grin, looked elsewhere as he always did, Jamie not knowing that he always looked off, away, because he was hopelessly—senselessly, he told himself—smitten by her fawnlike eyes, her chiseled features, the fineness of her bones and hands, by the way she carried herself with an outrageous effortlessness that had everything to do with a grace that had nothing imperious about it. So Galen looked off, pondered without her realizing that he knew this was the first time they had spoken directly to one another and that he was insane to attach any meaning to such a meaningless exchange, waited for Margaret to return with two iced teas and a mug of steaming coffee.

I could use a cup of coffee, Jamie said wistfully to the dog that was now lying at one end of the swept porch, so I'd better get a move on. The dog got to its feet at the sound of her voice, and she brought her hand to her brow, scanned the skies. The hawks were gone. She brought the dog into the house and checked her pocket for the five-dollar bill, took her empty knapsack, locked the door behind her, walked through the drive's snow and stepped onto the plowed lane, began the descent toward the reservoir road. As she made her way down, the pickup with poacher spotlights, a dented plow now mounted on its front end, strained up the hill toward her. Catch you on the way back, the driver yelled as he passed her by.

When she heard the truck slow behind her, she kept to its passenger side. The driver tooted, and she stopped for it to pass but the pickup stopped altogether, the driver leaning over in the cab and pushing open the door, then straightening back against his seat and revving the engine, looking at her the while, his expression contemptuous.

Get in for chrissakes, he yelled at her.

No, that's okay—

Get *in,* he bawled, I ain't got all day. And there was something in his eyes that held her, something in his eyes that made her climb into the cab. The pickup rode high, the shotgun in the rack even higher.

Name's Harlan, he said as if he were spewing a threat. Jamie did not respond, did not look at him, listened to the engine whine as they rolled down the lane in low gear, glanced at the beer cans rolling about her feet, noted the eyeless doll's head propped in the ashtray, took in the decals of naked women decorating the dashboard, the dice hanging from the rearview mirror. The windshield had a stonepock.

He drove with one hand on the wheel, one on the shift. So, you're Margaret's housekeeper, he told her, I heard about you. Where you going?

She looked at him: dark eyes set close, a gaunt face. A violence barely disguised. Down, she said.

Nah, not down. Wrong answer, not good enough. You get to come plowing with me for losing.

You can drop me here, she told him as the reservoir road came into sight.

Harlan laughed a harsh, guttural sound, pushed the truck into a higher gear, careened onto the reservoir road. Sit back and enjoy the ride, he said. We got a bit of business to take care of.

I don't have time—

Something tells me, Harlan cut her off, you got nothing but time. Now sit back like I said. And can it.

She held on to the edge of the seat, stared out the passenger window, knew it was crazy to even try to reach for the doorhandle. Harlan slowed before the junkman's drive and turned into it, lowered the plow, the snow resisting and the pickup lurching, him driving with both hands, leaning forward as if willing the give that came hard beneath the plow. Jamie braced herself, one hand now on the cab's ceiling and the other on the dashboard, and at the top of the drive Harlan whooped and ground down the gears and pushed on toward the junkman who stood beyond the drive's uppermost end. Harlan pulled the handbrake, left the engine running, and without so much as a word got out and walked to the end of his plowing. The junkman humped over onto the drive and the two men stood close to one another, talked at their feet, Harlan's back to the pickup. The junkman raised his head and nodded in her direction. When they came over to the truck, Harlan climbed into the cab as the junkman peered at her through the windshield. Jamie turned her head, looked away from him, saw the dead buck strung from a huge maple in the distance.

I was right about us having business, Harlan told her. He says you seen his boy.

She stared at the deer in its perfect stillness, aware of her breathing and of the two men watching her, did not respond. Harlan rapped his knuckles on the back of her head and she ducked, raised an arm that he caught by the wrist, held tightly.

He says you ain't living at Damon's no more. That you and your mutt and his boy are holed up somewhere together. He wants to know where.

She pulled free, glared at him.

I'm waiting. You ain't exactly being quick with any answers. And I thought you didn't have time.

He can say anything he likes, she told him.

Harlan hooted. You hear that, Jake?

The junkman narrowed his eyes, worked his mouth, leaned over, spit, straightened, said: Bitch.

Later, Harlan told him and, pushing in the clutch, reversed down the drive, raised the plow. Say the word, tell me where, he said as he backed onto the reservoir road.

The Four Corners, Jamie replied.

That ain't what I mean.

Search the quonset hut, she told him. And he made that guttural sound again, then whistled loudly, tunelessly, as the pickup spun recklessly on around the reservoir and over the causeway. When Harlan braked at The Four Corners, Jamie went for the door, but he reached the handle before she did, pinned her.

I didn't get your name, he told her, his face close. She breathed in his taint, drew back, said: Let me out. When he finally pulled on the handle and the door opened, her feet hit the ground hard.

You better bring the boy back if you know what's good for you and that mutt, he called out after her.

∽

That's bad company you're keeping, Jamie Hall.

She leaned her forehead against her empty mailbox, closed her eyes, straightened, locked it.

I'm not keeping company.

Good, the postmaster remarked, he's from bad stock. Trash. His father's people used to make moonshine years back, but they drank more than they sold.

His mother's people did worse.

He gave me a ride, that's all. I don't even know him.

Well, then, I'll tell you: he's a poacher. Me, I've never understood hunting, not leastwise poaching. To kill an animal hypnotized by a beam of light at night is hardly sport, and I know for a fact he's killed fawns and fallow deer just for their forelegs, taken young bucks for their tails. City folks used to buy such things, trophies for their walls, deer legs with thermometers on them, deer tails, buck heads if their rack of horns was impressive. That's pretty much over now, demand's petered out. These days he just plows some in the winter, mostly poaches for himself and the junkman's family, which he counts among the only relatives he has.

Now there's a clan, the postmaster went on, bound to misery and mayhem. Always was, being aberrant in their ways and given only to themselves, even in those times when they collected and traded mostly what no one needed. They were like vultures, breeding among themselves and perched up there on that ridge before the valley got flooded, squabbling over rot; what's left of them is still there, even more perverse now that there's nothing for them to do and hasn't been for a generation or two.

He paused, his head tremulous. She walked over to him, touched the back of one of his mottled hands. The mail's in, I take it.

He looked down at her slender fingers. It is, he told her. And then went to the door after she was gone, opened it, inhaled deeply, felt the cold eat into his frail chest, the pain course through his shoulder and arm, watched as she went into the convenience store. Wherein she broke the five-dollar bill into change, ignoring the cashier's scowl, went to the phone in the store's corner, dialed the operator and pushed the coins into the slot as the operator connected her to Margaret's number. There was no answering machine, no answer after the tenth ring. Jamie placed the receiver onto the hook and retrieved the returned coins that clattered into the phone's metal chamber, went through the aisles.

Check come? the cashier asked meanly before she rang up the purchases, disapproving of the change Jamie placed on the counter in payment. After bagging the groceries the cashier folded her arms and watched Jamie unhurriedly repack the cans of dogfood and coffee into her knapsack, discard the bag. The postmaster was still standing in the doorway when she came out of the store and, not casting a glance in his direction, walked toward the road with that rhythmic lightness he had never forgotten. And then she was gone, vanishing into a hard season, one that would get harder, making her way toward the causeway that he could still remember seeing from the reservoir's middle, standing on that ice he'd worked so carelessly, recklessly, when he was no longer young and not yet old—reckless because the only woman he had ever loved, desired without a declaration, would never be his, was already another's, careless because he'd come to understand the relentless contempt of those empty years stretching before him, that he would be lonelier than he already was. He could still picture the cutting tools and great pincers, the sleighs piled high with iceblocks, the teams of horses straining and sometimes losing their footing and always wearing blinders so they wouldn't shy at the sight of the water that gushed black into the holes from which the blocks were cut—the now aged postmaster at that time younger, too close to the edge of those holes—or at the bonfires, the pyres, the workers made to warm themselves. He had been a reckless man then, careless upon the ice, captured in photographs he had in a shoebox somewhere, photographed serious and unsmiling and mourning his unrequited passion, icepick in hand and with a hat set roguishly on his head, among his fellow workers. And he could see himself too as he was now, old beyond even his own recognition, and foolish, yes, foolish, he scolded himself, to be so taken by this girl who was in every way the spitting image of her grandmother.

He promised himself that he'd find that box of photographs to give to her—he had no one else—and stared down the road in that wintry season, thought: How cruel to have lived this long, to see the past return.

Nine

Galen found the drive plowed, and he swallowed back the bitter taste that erupted in his mouth at the thought that Harlan—whom Margaret would never hire, for she had no use for anyone plowing since she was here only in summer and otherwise had no use for Harlan at all— had been there and cleared the way to the top of the property: he would be back to poach. When Galen reached the house he heard the dog bark from inside, set the four teardrop-shaped catgut snowshoes—the pair he'd worn, and the pair he had carried—against the porch rail, saw that Jamie had not touched the deer meat. He waited. When she finally appeared at the top of the lane, there was a tiredness to her gait.

Just in time for coffee, she said by way of greeting when she reached the porch.

I could use some, he replied, watching her take in

the snowshoes and knowing that second pair spoke volumes. For as soon as Jamie saw them she knew that Galen already knew there was more to her being at Margaret's than there had ever been. The dog came to him after she opened the door, and Galen petted it as she brought out two stools and set them on the porch before going back inside, reappearing a short time later with two steaming mugs. They sat and cupped their hands around these, let the strong brew warm them. Galen eventually put his cup down, stretched out a leg, reached into a pocket and came up with tobacco, rolled a cigarette. He smoked half of it, thinking of Damon in Dyers Corner two nights' back, splay-elbowed in front of a row of empty shot glasses on the bar, gazing drunkenly at his reflection in the bar's mirror—which was cracked and long unwashed, lined with faded polaroids of red-eyed people staring out of them and with eagle-and-flag decals—with his wife next to him, her pale, somber, pretty face slightly puffy, a roundness already claiming her waist.

So, Galen finally remarked, you're here.

Jamie said nothing.

You should have left him months ago.

I'm not sure I'm the one who left, she pronounced thoughtfully, keeping her profile to Galen.

Appearances to the contrary, he said.

Galen wondered whether Jamie knew that Damon's

wife was pregnant. He smoked the rest of the cigarette in silence, pondered the sky's unbroken overcast, felt the weight of the winter to come in his bones. The dog nosed at her when Galen rose and walked to the porch's end to extinguish it, and she placed a palm on the dog's head and met Galen's eyes when he turned around. Well, the worst of it is, he said, as much to the dog as to her, it's lonely up here.

The worst of it, Galen, is that it's lonely everywhere.

He knew that to be true.

At any rate, he told her, that meat should last you a while. I can butcher it, pack it up for the freezer. Or you can hack at it.

I don't even know how to cook deer.

In that case, I'll take over kitchen duty.

He slipped out of his jacket and walked behind her, put it about her shoulders, took the deer meat down from the wisteria, undid his boots and stepped out of them, went inside and closed the door behind him. She did not put her arms through the sleeves but pulled the jacket close around her, breathing in his sweet mansweat smell, his tobacco-and-woodsmoke scent, wondered at the impossibility of ever knowing what it was to be someone else, to wear another's skin, be inside someone else, know another's heart; and she watched the day darken and the first spit of thin sleet fall. When Galen returned he took their mugs and then brought her another cup of coffee, stood for a while as wet snow began to mix with the sleet, remarked: You'll catch your death if you sit out here much longer.

I'll be in in a while, she said. And after a while, when she finally entered the house, the odor of stewing meat—not sweet, almost rank, something of hemlock or bark about it—permeated the downstairs. She found Galen standing before Margaret's photographs, hands humbly clasped before him like a penitent within some ex-voto niche. She went and stood near—too near—him, moved along the wall with him as he studied Margaret's chronicle of places and people Jamie did not know. He paused before a photograph of bear cubs caught in midair on tire swings, in front of others: before an eyepatched boy grinning widely between two other boys whose shadowed expressions were serious, before a merry-go-round whose gilded horses were arrested in varying stages of gallop, their carved manes falsely flowing and nostrils flared and eyes rolled back and tails lifted high above bunched haunches, before geese waddling through sunlight in front of a miniature gingerbread house that straddled a muddied stream as a child clutched a mustachioed rabbit, before a cat draped over the edge of a flatroofed wrenhouse. Galen studied a photograph of a kneeling boy kissing a lamb, the boy's eyes raised to the man standing before him with his back to the camera, shook his head, said: I don't remember that day.

Jamie looked at him in surprise, and he nodded. That's me. Once upon a time.

She could not see the boy in the man. Nor the man in the boy.

How we change, he remarked. You can't recognize yourself from one age to another. This, he continued, tapping a finger on the glass, is my father. I remember that shirt, his hat.

You've known Margaret since you were a boy?

Since forever. Mostly she used to come and go, but for a while it seemed like she was always there, wherever my father was. I've never asked whether they were more than friends—she was older than he was, there were other things as well—but they spent some time together. Margaret always carrying her cameras, lugging around her tripod, always wearing khaki pants and a vest with lots of pockets, with a scarf around her neck. Red, or yellow. Huh. It was a long time ago.

And what is this place?

My father's dream. In the end, probably his nightmare. An animal farm, with pens of domesticated everything. He thought people would come, that parents would bring their children to feed the deer, watch the bears, pet the sheep, the rabbits, stroke the ducks—no one could get near the geese—gather hen eggs, examine turtles, picnic, ride the merry-go-round that broke down more often than not, try the ponies. Pay the admission fee. To this day, Galen added pensively, I don't know what he was thinking. It's in the middle of nowhere.

It's still there?

In a way. Falling apart, rundown.

And your father?

Galen shook his head. No, there's only me now. Ventured: What about you?

Jamie moved away from him, wrapped her arms about her, stopped before the photograph of the grinning eyepatched boy between two boys on either side of him. It's you, she finally said, pointing him out. And who are they?

Galen stayed where he was. The one with the patch is, was, Bobby Sanders, he answered. The other one is someone called Harlan.

꙳

After Jamie told Galen about Harlan and the junkman, about the boy, she sat on the floor with her legs crossed, watched the flames in the fireplace shoot sparks upward into the draft, ate the stew Galen brought as wordlessly as a suppliant. The dog sat attentively at her side as she picked at the meat that tasted of wilder-

ness, followed Galen when he took her empty plate and
returned with more; but she shook her head and then
Galen went back into the kitchen, gave to the dog what
Jamie had refused. She did not say goodnight, but Galen
heard her get up, the stairs creak. He waited for her to
come back down, and when she did not he washed and
dried the dishes, wiped down the kitchen counter, went
back to the fireplace to find the blaze reduced to glowing
coals. He put on a log, two, which caught slowly and
then flared, sucking the thin warmth from the room.

Happy new year, he said to the dog. And then he
stretched out on the rug fully dressed, disturbed by and
fully aware of her presence, drifted into an uneasy twilight sleep, slept. When the dog later woke him by
pawing and whining at the door, the fire was down to a
smoldering topography of minute and myriad ridges
embedded in ash. He shushed the dog to quiet it, but the
dog pawed, whined more loudly, so that Galen got up
and unshuttered a window, looked out into the spectral
night. Dull moonlight silvered behind the clouds, and in
the now-thin snowfall the boy, phantasmagoric, raised
his arms and spun circles in front of the orchard.

⌐

Galen opened his eyes, waking to the smell of cold
ashes and charred wood and to the strangeness of the

house, rose stiffly from the floor and felt exhausted from collaring the dog with one hand the night long. He went into the kitchen, careful to not disturb the silence, the dog on his heels, and heated the leftover coffee. When the pot began to sizzle he cut the flame and poured a mug and wandered about, here and there sluicing open the shutters onto the diffuse gray dawn, assessed the snow's accumulation and judged it little enough not to warrant plowing. Despite avoiding the wall of photographs, Galen was unable to stop thinking of that photograph of Harlan and himself, serious and unsmiling on either side of Bobby Sanders.

Bobby had always come between them. Galen wondered whether Margaret had intuited that, had posed them with Bobby—his eyepatch string twisted—in the middle; more likely, he mused, it's just the way they were. A year and some had passed between the time Bobby Sanders had lost his eye and Margaret had pressed the shutter button more than twenty years before, Galen couldn't say exactly when; but he remembered the day Bobby Sanders blinded himself as though no time had elapsed at all. *There ain't nothing to killing, there just ain't nothing to it,* Bobby was telling him and Harlan that morning as the sun warmed their backs and they squatted at the edge of that newly paved road, spread not with macadam but with a rough asphalt

amalgam that had pieces of quartz in it, the quartz glit-
tering like what they imagined to be huge diamond
chunks, the three of them digging out those chunks
from the curb lipping onto the grass by the telephone
pole. The flies were slow and stupid, not yet warmed by
the sun, and they caught them and watched Bobby pull
them apart before squishing them with his father's
switchblade, the same they were using to dig out the
quartz. And after they tired of killing flies, after their
pockets were bulging with quartz, they began flipping the
knife at the pole so that it would hit tip first, Bobby going
on about how they'd catch frogs later and put firecrackers
in their mouths and blow them to smithereens as he sent
the blade flying through the air and it boomeranged back,
caught him square in his eye, his mouth going oval and
him screaming and running and pulling at that knife so
that when it fell out his eyeball did too.

It was Harlan who picked up the impaled eye, which
had something like a bloody tail and was round as a ball;
but it was Bobby Sanders's crazy old man who kept that
thing in a jar of formaldehyde somewhere and one day
gave it to Bobby like a prize the first time he and Harlan
and Galen returned from porcupine hunting with
Bobby's new beebee gun, coming back with three noses
worth two dollars each from the fish and game people.
Bobby's father just handed the jar to his son then,

saying, If anybody ever says you need more'n one eye to shoot straight with, you just show 'em this and tell 'em you got both your eyes. And then he'd made pancakes drenched with syrup, and Bobby put the jar on the table and they ate staring at his eyeball. Only Galen had retched, which caused Bobby and Harlan to exclude him when they slit open their thumbs and mingled their blood later on that afternoon, probably sealing their fates and for the worse by doing so.

Sealed his fate too, Galen knew. For the boy standing ethereal in the night, haunting her who had untied him, meant one thing and one thing only to Galen: Harlan.

Or so he told Jamie when he returned from walking far beyond the orchard that morning, with the dog dolphin-leaping through the snow toward her after not losing the boy's scent but not following it either, Galen seeing despite last night's thin, fresh fall the boy's trail leading to the forest and down through the woods before he and the dog turned back. She stood watching from the porch their shadowless approach under a tin sky, bluish circles about her sleepless eyes.

I think—no, I know, Galen said to her, the boy was here. Last night.

Why?

I don't know, Galen replied. I don't know why he's wandering around anywhere, never mind here. But I'm going to find Harlan.

Why?

Because I need to know what he knows, why he's looking for the boy. Because Harlan will be back up here the next snowfall, or the one after that, as soon as it's deep enough to plow, as soon as he figures the deer are hungry enough to start pawing around the orchard and make his poaching easy.

He knows I'm the housekeeper—

But he doesn't know you're *here*. And I don't want him to figure that out, not if the boy is coming around, leaving tracks everywhere. If that happens, Harlan will think what the junkman already believes.

She made a strangled sound, brought a hand to her mouth, dropped it, said in an almost inaudible voice. I'll come with you.

No. No, you won't.

I can't just—

Yes you can. You just stay inside, stay here. And wait.

For what?

For me, he told her.

Ten

Morning drew the boy downward under cinder-colored clouds behind which the sun remained hidden, and when he reached the forest's edge beyond the pigsty he climbed into a tree and sat unmoved by and unmoving within time's flow, watched in its listless passing Ada and the man who was his father and the man he knew was called Harlan muck through the charred debris of what was once the shed. The silence among them was broken only by the grunts of the sow that lay hogtied on its side, which the three ignored. The two men poked at the remains of the shed with shovels, the woman with a stick, and on occasion the men would drag the remnants of a fired beam or a length of metal out from the rubble. Whether they turned up pieces of bone the boy did not—could not—know, or care, and he waited the wait of the uncurious as the men shoveled snowsoaked

charcoal and ash into an old barrel and then rolled it to
the edge of a shallow pit they'd managed to excavate
from the frozen earth and dumped the contents, the wet
ash not sporing, just settling like sludge.

The boy picked at the lint and crumbs in the frayed
linings of his pockets and licked his fingers and made no
other movement until he climbed down, following some
instinct to which he gave no thought. When he reached
a stream not entirely frozen he plunged into it and
stumbled along in the water like an agitated animal
intent upon leaving no trace of its scent. From time to
time he paused in the stream's frigidity, watched
screaming jays bluestreak before him in flight. Some distance from the stream he scrambled out and circled
back toward the junkyard, toward the clapboard house,
broke into a leaden lope with earflaps raised and hat
askew and soaked to his knees, ran past Harlan's spat-
tered pickup truck, past the strung buck, the listing
sheds. He slowed on the trodden, icy path that led
through the house's yard, in the midst of which the
mute stood drooling, his hands limp at his sides and his
pants undone, rocking slowly from foot to foot. From
within the house, a child wailed.

The boy raised his fist to the mute, and once inside
the house breathed in the smell of rot and creosote,
found on the unlit stove a mess of beans coagulated

around a slab of saltpork and ate hand to mouth, scraping his broken fingernails along the pot's insides for the last crust of beanmold. When finished he pushed at the unwashed dishes in the sink, threw plates to the floor, pumped water and brought his mouth to the flow, drank his fill as the wet oozed from his boots and puddled the floor. And then the boy knocked about and, giving vent to some manic rampage that silenced the howling child, tore through the house overturning chairs, kicking at doors, ripping from the beds fouled blankets and from the wallpegs stained shirts, useless horsebits, leather straps, unmended sweaters, the pegs from the wall.

He found his sibling on the floor and tied to a bedpost, the child's mouth twisted, eyes and nose running, leaning into its harness and taut against its tether. And the boy wavered then as though trying to recall something until he fixated on the harness, set about trying to undo the tether's knot. When he could not he lifted the leg of the bedpost and slipped the line free and tugged at the child, whose head jerked back and then forward as he fell upon his stomach and pushed himself up onto his hands and knees, rocked himself into a crawl. The boy tugged again, this time with a vicious snap, and the child sprawled forward into the drag and let out a scream, bobbed along the floor as the boy pulled it from the room. When the child caught on a doorjamb, the boy lifted his sibling by the back of the harness and the child gasped for breath between cries as its head and limbs flailed downward. The boy strode through the littered house, yanking the child behind him, unheedful of his sibling's distress. Outside, the mute made strange gurgling sounds, ponderously shuffled from foot to foot, and gazed at nothing, neither following the boy's retreat nor flinching at the resounding shot and the blood-curdling squeal of the dying sow.

Eleven

Galen paused and looked skyward, knowing more snow would fall, heavy, wet, over the wilderness he snowshoed through, and he gauged his pace as much by the look of the sky as by the miles he had left to go. The air was damp and cold and he was glad for both, and for the pungent aroma of pine and spruce and cedar as he wound his way through dense swatches of fir. He followed a barely discernible trail that snaked endlessly through lower reaches of the mountain range and stretched like a thin thread, here broken, there knotted, for unimaginable distances. Galen knew this part of the trail and the landscape it traversed, days and days of it; and though he could not tell its measure in length he knew its meanderings in time, how many hours from a certain hollow to a certain craggy crest, from an abandoned well to a certain oak, how many days to a two-pinnacled pass.

Just below a bald ridge Galen cut away from the trail, slowed over a slide of snowburied bluestone scree, caught a deerpath that wound down along a long stone wall that separated forest from forest and no longer demarcated with any meaning whatever it had once existed for, some logical purpose now best speculated upon by asylum-dwellers. The day, the light, was much like the last day Galen had ever spent with Harlan, had ever seen Harlan, the sun not exposing itself and the cold fierce and moist, the sky low and layered with a cloudcover that seemed to warp, undulate. Bobby Sanders was in his grave for some six months by then, buried seven weeks before Galen had returned for good from the service, only knowing at first what everyone knew, that Bobby had been drunk when he shot himself. Afterward knowing what Harlan told him, that Bobby was drunk and crazed, drunk because he was crazed and crazed because he was lovesick—Harlan's word, Galen not believing it, Galen knowing that Bobby was capable of obsession, of fixation, but not of love—but whether lovesick, obsessed, or fixated, incapable in any case of reining in his lust for a voluptuously wide, sloe-eyed, dimwitted creature whose father gave her to Bobby to do with whatever he wanted whenever Bobby had a few bucks in his pockets to spare or a few pints of hard liquor to trade. And Bobby wanting everything, doing everything, there being nothing she would not do and there being nothing that Bobby couldn't get her to do for a few bonbons, so that it was only a matter of time before he couldn't stay away and only a matter of time before he trespassed, trampled upon, all limits, got her to do things to him and to let him do things to her— sometimes with her old man watching and at other times with Harlan watching and sometimes sharing her with Harlan—because she was compliant and uncomprehending, and therefore shameless, no matter what. Had Bobby brought half the male population of Dyers Corner to join him, she would have acquiesced and thought nothing of it, thought of nothing but the bonbons—or so Harlan told Galen. Except that her old man remarked that fact first. When Bobby heard about that he bludgeoned her father almost to death, not only in full view of his hapless daughter but as Harlan lay her bellydown over a table and made her mewl. That, Harlan said, probably saved the old man's life, because Bobby stopped beating him the moment she began to make that weird catlike sound, she who had never so much as even sucked in her breath or sighed no matter what Bobby had ever done to her. It stopped Bobby in his tracks, so startled him that his mouth dropped open and his one eye widened to show white all around, and then they left. They drank hard, Harlan barely keeping up, until they ended up sitting across from each other at a kitchen table with a revolver and a fifth between them, each of them spinning the bottle and slugging from it whenever the mouth pointed at one or the other. Bobby in the end spinning the revolver too, saying *She loves me she loves me not* and gazing at the revolver's rotation until something in him snapped, until he picked up the gun and grinned at Harlan and said *She loves me not* and brought it to his temple, pulled the trigger.

Or so Harlan told Galen. That and: I'm taking care of her in my own way. I'm taking care of her, and I'm gonna take care of her. You see if I don't.

In the end he took care of her once and for all, she who could not have loved anyone and who six months after Bobby was in his grave no longer even knew who he was or had been. She who Galen could not remember clearly, though he still had an impression of abundant flesh barely contained by a thin coat, of a kerchief knotted under an ample chin, of plump wrists and doughy hands and thick calves and stubby wide feet in tightfitting, skinthin ankle boots, her mouth full, round, her eyes wideset. She was sitting in the jalopy Harlan was driving, that first and last time Galen met her, when Harlan pulled to the side of the road where Galen was waiting for him, rifle in hand and ready to hunt, to chase away the morning doing what they'd planned. Galen saying: You can't be serious.

C'mon, Harlan told him, put the gun in the back and get in.

She can't come with us, Harlan, Galen protested as the engine idled with a clanking sound and a noxious white cloud spewed from the muffler, Galen shifting the rifle from one hand to the other, stomping his feet in the cold.

So we won't do much hunting. We'll picnic instead.

You're crazy. Count me out.

Aw, you're gonna upset her, Harlan whined. And then she leaned her head forward, craned her neck, looked at Galen from underneath painted eyelids, her eyeliner too thick, crooked, her mouth a round red smear, and Harlan elbowed her and she lifted the paperbag she was holding on her lap and smiled a slow smile at Galen.

That's okay, Galen told her, thanks anyway. It's just not quite picnic weather.

Bobby took you on picnics all the time, didn't he? Harlan cooed at her. Even in winter, right? Right?

I don't know, she mumbled.

Sure you do. You remember.

She gazed at Galen, the bag still in midair, asked: Are you Bobby?

Harlan doubled over the steering wheel, hit it with the heels of his hands as he came up. Picnics—are—

nice, she told Galen, and Harlan yelled Jesusfreaking-
christ man just get *in,* and then Galen put his rifle in the
back and got in, with her between them in the front and
thigh to thigh with both of them and Galen pushing
himself against the door, shaking his head, saying, She'll
freeze, and Harlan just driving and sometimes chucking
her under the chin and singing in a falsetto *I wanna be
Bobby's girl, I wanna be Bobby's girl,* until Galen told him
to cut it out, exasperated, not yet feeling uneasy: that
came later, on the way through the woods to what they
called the ledges, Galen carrying the rifle—just in case,
man, Harlan had argued, and besides you don't wanna
leave it in the car, somebody'll come by and bust in—
and leading the way and Harlan whistling *I wanna be
Bobby's girl,* alerting any wildlife within a five-mile
radius to their presence; no, the intense unease came
later, after she began sniffling, started stumbling, after
Harlan took Galen's gloves so his hands wouldn't freeze
every time he pulled her out of the snow and to her feet,
when Harlan smacked her into wailing and her tears
streaked her makeup and Harlan began pushing,
herding her from behind as she plodded toward Galen
with something like ponderous bovine grace, if that's
what grace is, clutching the paperbag and crying: I
wanna go back now. I wanna go back.

I've had enough, Galen told Harlan then, feeling

more fearful than he'd ever felt in his life. Told him: I'm
going back.

Aw hell Galen, we're almost there for chrissakes,
Harlan insisted, pushing at her angrily, himself huffing.
And then Galen tramped off, left them behind, reached
the ledges and set the rifle buttend down, waited for
them and moved about to stay warm, blew into his
hands, cupped them beneath his armpits, cursing himself and feeling not only anxious but irritated too, so
irritated that when she and Harlan got to the ledges and
Harlan took the bag from her and tossed it in Galen's
direction, Galen kept his hands where they were, made
no attempt to catch it, so that she lurched forward and,
retrieving the bag from the ground, clutched it to her
chest and for no reason Galen could think of simply
went as far as she could go, until her nose just about hit
a ledge, and then turned around. Galen saying: Harlan,
what the hell—because Harlan suddenly had the rifle up
to his shoulder and her in the sights.

So where's Bobby now, huh? Harlan taunted her,
Where's Bobby now? He swung the barrel in Galen's
direction when Galen took a step toward him, told
Galen to stay where he was, beaded on her again. Neither she nor Galen understanding what Harlan was getting at—never mind meant—by raising his voice,
repeating, So where's Bobby now, huh? Where's Bobby?

She caught on a sob, blubbered, I don't know no Bobby.

I don't know no Bobby, I don't know nobody, Harlan echoed hatefully.

Noooooo.

Noooooo, Harlan mimicked. Noooooo. Well he's in his grave, that's where he is, he screamed at her. So whaddaya think of that?

I dunno, she bawled, I dunno, she sobbed. I—like—picnics.

This ain't no picnic—

Harlan, stop—

Shut up! *Shut up!* Harlan yelled at Galen. She made Bobby crazy, she turned him inside out, twisted him into—

He was always twisted—

Says you, Harlan cried, and you don't know shit, you don't know how she drove him nuts, him just not being able to get enough of her, all that fat, all that flesh, all that mouth and ass and him killing himself because—

I don't know no Bobby, she wailed.

Cunt, Harlan said, pulled the trigger.

The shot propelled her backward against the ledge, and as she crumpled Galen thought he would never stop screaming and then he did and was upon her, her keeling over and him pulling at her coat, the snow bloodying and Galen on his knees saying *ohmygod ohmygod ohmygod* and trying to staunch the bleeding, her kerchief still knotted and frothy clots bubbling out of her mouth and the stain on her chest seeping as the light leaked from her eyes, and then Galen was alone with her, alone with the gun and the gloves Harlan had dropped, no longer uneasy or irritated or even scared, just numb, in shock lying by her side and listening to his own pulse throb in his ears, colder than he had ever been. He closed his eyes and did not regain consciousness until strangers with male voices began to pull him to his feet, Galen hardly able to stand and beginning to pass out again as Harlan said, Oh man I don't know what happened, I was too far behind them. Someone else exclaimed: *Sonovabitch.*

When Galen came to, he was in the backseat of a car between two men. They followed the county ambulance a good way before Galen slipped back into shock, again closed his eyes.

⌒

By the time Galen broke out onto the road above the spillway, a damp snow was falling lightly. He took off the snowshoes, strapped them onto his back, went on. No one drove by him on the road, which wound about in ways he did not remember, and beyond the spillway he began to wonder whether what he'd heard about where Harlan's place was might have been nothing but hearsay, kept wondering until he saw the pickup with its poacher lights in front of a shingled house missing almost as many shingles as it had.

Galen stood the snowshoes against the truck, went to the house, rapped on its flimsy door. The slovenly woman who opened it clutched the waist of a faded housecoat with one hand, held a beer in the other. Galen did not know her. He asked for Harlan and gave his name and she closed the door on him. He heard Harlan's voice from somewhere inside, took another breath, kicked the snow from his boots, brushed it from his shoulders and hood. When Harlan opened the door, he said: Shit.

Harlan.

Well, shit, Harlan said again. I guess you might as well come in.

They moved through a cramped kitchen, with its shellacked plywood cupboards and a ratty blue dishtowel strung across a dirty window, the only color in the room but for the lewd plastic magnets stuck to the refrigerator door, and down a narrow hall into a den. Harlan shoved aside a metal box of shells and rags and oilcans from a chair and sat on a hassock, took up the rifle he was cleaning. The woman was nowhere to be seen. Take a chair, Harlan told Galen, pushing a rod down the gun's barrel, seeing you're here.

Galen sat, waited, watched Harlan finish cleaning the rifle, click open its chamber, snap it shut, wipe down the wooden stock, watched him raise the gun, aim at a sidewall. Galen braced himself so as not to flinch.

So what brings you round, after all this time? Harlan asked. He shifted the gun and trained it on Galen, a twitch lifting the corner of his mouth. He cocked the lever, swung the barrel wide, pulled the trigger. Galen blinked at the hollow click.

A hunch.

What kinda hunch? That we're still buddies?

Not a chance.

Well, what?

I thought you might know something about the junkman's boy.

Harlan's eyes narrowed. You seen him?

Now, that's a dead giveaway.

I ain't said nothing.

Maybe I have seen him, Galen said.

Harlan put the rifle across his knees, shifted on the hassock.

Does that interest you, Harlan?

It might.

Well, Galen said as he stood up, when you figure it

out whether it does or not—

Hang on, Harlan told him, Galen already in the doorway. Just sit back down. C'mon, take a seat. Tell me what you're up to these days.

Galen leaned against the doorframe. I didn't come to pay a social visit, he said.

Aw, for chrissakes, I'm interested. I heard you're trapping some.

You heard right.

Whereabouts?

Around.

That ain't too specific.

No.

How'd you know where to find me?

I hear things too, Galen told him.

Yeah, I bet. How'd you hear about the boy?

So long, Galen said, turning to leave.

Wait. Wait, dammit, I'll make you a deal.

And Galen stopped, walked back to the doorway, leaned against its frame again. I'll make you a deal, Harlan repeated. You tell me, I'll tell you.

Tell you what?

If you saw him.

I saw him.

You see anything else?

Like what?

I'm asking.

Me too.

Harlan snorted. Been a long time, Galen. Bygones is bygones, I assume.

Don't assume anything. You said a deal, so this is the deal: you tell me what's going on, and I'll tell you where I saw him.

That's not much of a deal.

It's the only one you're getting.

Harlan cursed, relented. Okay, I'll tell you this much, Harlan said. The boy's not right in his head.

That's no surprise, considering where's he's from.

Says you.

You looking for him, Harlan?

What's it to you?

If you're not, I'm just wasting my time, Galen told him, pulling his hood over his head.

Hang on, Harlan protested. Okay. I'm looking for him.

Why?

Call it a favor.

You've never done a favor in your life.

Bullshit I ain't.

You never did me any. And you owe me one.

I don't owe you shit. And then Harlan squirmed, said, Aw, fuck it, it's like this: the boy's been raising hell around the junkyard.

Meaning.

The details ain't rightly your business.

But they're yours?

It's a family thing, private like. Blood being thicker than water, no matter how thin, and Ada being about the only relation I've got that I happen to know of, no matter how distant.

Tell me what's going on.

Tell me, tell me, Harlan sneered. Okay, let me repeat: the kid's loony. And I'll tell you one more thing: he disappears, comes back, trashes the place, sets fire to things.

But Jake and Ada want him back anyway.

Well, let's just say they don't much feel like being asleep when he gets around to paying his next visit.

Then maybe you should get the sheriff to protect them, Galen remarked, unless you're hanging as much as you poach out at their place. Unless you're not on the terms I remember you being with the sheriff. Or unless you don't want him to start figuring out why the boy's wandering around in the middle of winter, as if bad weather is better than a warm house. Or why someone tied him up to a tree and why that boy decided that being loose and staying loose was a fine idea probably just as soon as he got untied.

Well, I'll be damned, Harlan pronounced, I'll be

damned.

Of that I've no doubt.

So where is she?

Who?

That girl that untied him. The one who cleans at Margaret's, the only one who could've told you about the boy being tied. Damon's tramp.

Galen shot Harlan a warning look that made him howl. Oh sweet jesus, Galen, you getting a piece of her? Is that it? You seen that boy 'cause she's got him somewhere and got you sniffing around her like a dog?

I saw him, Galen said evenly, in the northwest corner of the reservoir.

Like hell you did.

Then I'm mistaken.

Sorely, Harlan muttered, trying to discern from Galen's unreadable expression whether he was telling the truth. Then asked: Exactly when?

Two nights back.

Harlan thought about that. What the hell, he shrugged, could be. He's been back to the house since.

How recently?

Yesterday morning. Tore the place up, took something he shouldn't of.

I can imagine.

No you can't.

Galen closed the top clasp on his jacket. Hey, Harlan
said.

What?

You see that boy again, you snatch him. Bring him
back to the junkyard, or bring him here. And do it real
fast if you're mixed up with that girl who's mixed up in
this herself and who I know ain't at Damon's anymore.

Give me one good reason why.

Because I'm itching for a good hunt. Because when
I catch up to her, you won't like it one bit.

⤷

Uneasy again, troubled by Harlan's transparent
malevolence and his own sense of futility, Galen back-
tracked his way to Margaret's, the snow falling heavier
now and him reflecting upon that sealed fate which in
and of itself had not put him in prison—for Galen had
made choices back then, not so much choosing to protect Harlan as he always had, but choosing not to protect
himself because he had not prevented what had happened and was in his own eyes guilty of, if not passivity,
then disbelief. Galen never claimed his innocence, never
said that the shooting was a mishap—not that anyone
would have believed him, given how clear it was that she
was no more than five yards away and that the rifle had
to have been pointed straight at her and hadn't dis-

charged at any angle that could have indicated an accident—but he did steadfastly maintain that he could not
remember what had happened, said he couldn't plead
innocence or guilt, told the court-appointed lawyer that
not only didn't he want a jury trial but that he didn't
even want the lawyer to make a motion for bail, which
Galen's father, already in the county's VA hospital with
the phlebitis that would eventually kill him, could not
have posted anyway. And so the prosecutor and judge
and lawyer had only Harlan's sworn, inexact testi-
mony—Harlan claimed he hadn't seen anything, but he
had theories—and the coroner's report. They distrusted
Harlan but could not doubt the coroner, or, it seemed,
Galen's insistent lack of recall. And then did what they
could—Harlan being suspect, and Galen being a young
man who had never broken any law so far as anyone
knew and who had done his military service and was a
local boy, a respected widower's son—the judge more
than agreeable to an uncontested plea bargain, sending
Galen to prison not for twenty-five to life for first-
degree murder but sentencing him to seven years for
manslaughter, the judge himself with more than a
gnawing doubt that justice had not been served and
breaking with precedent by asking to see Galen in his
chambers after pronouncing the sentence in order to tell
him that he had never in his life been so reluctant to

sentence anyone and that, given good behavior, Galen might be out in five years. Galen reflected now that those five years had stretched meaninglessly, emptily before him then, remembered how slowly the seasons came and went and how he had longed only for winters so that he could contemplate in each snowfall its random uniqueness.

And so Galen had waited out each spring summer fall in prison and in winter named the different snows that fell, distinguished the fineness or thickness of the flakes, the patterns in which they fell, the snow sometimes drizzling like frozen raindust and at other times spewing from the sky in curdled whorls or blinding sheets or with a cloying wetness or crystalline clarity; and each snowfall blanketed the prison yard and was trod upon by men whose footsteps were muffled in singular and peculiar ways by it, whose voices were hushed into murmur while milling about aimlessly on their daily exercise rounds in the quadrant, Galen not walking about but standing as if benumbed, his face lifted to the heavens so that the flakes might catch on the brim of his cap, on his eyelashes, as he marveled at no two flakes being alike and at the miracle that anything as unremarkable as the smallest raindrop could be transformed into something of such complicated, incalculable beauty. The winters were the only seasons that passed by quickly, Galen mostly watching from the patch of sky smallframed in his cell's barred window as each of the coldest months spent itself in one snowfall after another, the snow spitting or spilling and sometimes caught in iridescent snowshafts in the prison's searchlight beams at night.

No one had ever come, not in all those years. Not the girl Galen had already left behind when he came north after doing his service and whom he never expected to see again anyway. Not his father (don't, Galen told him, just take care of yourself) and not Margaret (don't, Galen told her, it's too humiliating and besides they'd never allow you to bring in your camera), who did not believe in sealed fates but who was all too familiar with deadly accidents, her small grandson having drowned the morning she hadn't stopped him from paddling away in a canoe by himself because she had assumed he'd done it before, assumed he swam well enough anyway. Galen's father wrote to him, Margaret wrote to him, but neither ever intimated to Galen, warned Galen, that his father was deteriorating, failing, never told him that Margaret was helping to pay the property taxes on that animal farm that had not been an animal farm since the day Galen and his father had given away the last of the sheep and unpenned the last of the deer, the deer following them to the office and then grazing before it and not at all heeding any call of the wild, neither of them mentioning that Margaret was helping out so that Galen would have somewhere to return to and neither ever hinting that his father for a fact would not survive to see that day. Which they knew, which is why Galen's father kept up the small life insurance policy he had and instructed his lawyer to use it after Galen's release to pay on an annual basis and for a decade those property taxes and put what was left over into a bank account in Galen's name. When Galen walked out of prison after five winters of naming snows and five springs summers autumns that crept by at a snail's pace, there was no one there to meet him, not the girl he hadn't forgotten but who was lost to him forever, not his father who could not rise from the grave, not Margaret who wrote to him that there was no such thing as fate, just coincidence and accident and each and every person's dogged will to persist in getting on with life despite its vagaries. Which prompted Galen to write back: Don't come. If you're right, I should be able to make my own way home.

Which he did. And without that uneasy feeling he'd experienced once, but which was now consuming him again as the thickfeathered snow fell without so much as a whisper. The farther he walked, the farther he got from Harlan, the more convinced Galen became that he was hopelessly entangled within some web, caught up by and fearful of fate, in a situation that seemed neither accidental nor coincidental and was certainly not of Galen's own creation.

⤺

Galen told Jamie what he knew, then added that he thought Harlan had not noticed the deer meat cached in the wisteria. She listened and ate little, said less, eventually stretched out on the rug before the fire and closed her eyes, the dog beside her. Galen sat in an armchair, watched the light flicker over her, dance upon the fineness of her bones, illumine her translucent skin, shine upon her thick, long hair, understood the longings of any voyeur.

Jamie, he finally said. He had never spoken her name aloud to her before.

She stirred and rubbed at her eyes, sat up, her face softened by sleep. Galen brought one socked foot up and caught it on the edge of the seat, leaned back into the chair, into his body's tiredness.

I'll be going tomorrow, Galen told her, as soon as Harlan plows, as soon as he's gone.

A log snapped behind her, sparks spewing and catching in the upward draft, and she craned her head to the side and watched them disappear into nothingness.

Galen rose and went to his knapsack, rummaged for tobacco, rolled a cigarette, then went over to the fireplace and lit the cigarette with an ember, sat on the floor with his back to the flames. He reached out tentatively, touched her wrist.

Come with me.

She saw him half-enshadowed, shook her head. I can't.

He considered what he might say to change her mind, realized he knew her so little that he had no idea where to begin. She interrupted his thoughts, said, I'll be going too.

When?

She shrugged.

And where will you go?

Somewhere else, she replied.

With the dog.

The dog is all I have.

He looked away from her, and the silence bled between them as though from a cavernous wound. He smoked, flicked the end of the cigarette into the fire, sighed. Tell me, he said then, about Damon.

Damon. She saw the causeway in the night, the fireflies hovering over the waters and far beneath the stars, knew herself to have been more alone at that moment than she'd ever imagined possible and more lonely for

the stranger behind the wheel nosing the car into the
orbed light of its headlamps, her with nowhere to go
and going nowhere. There's nothing to tell, she
remarked, guarding within her memories of the airless
attic room once upon a time painted some brilliant
shade of yellow long since faded and with one unshaded
lightbulb, under which they first made love; keeping
deep within her recollections of Damon's comings and
goings, his erratic ways and those errant days that came
and went, melding into weeks, months, Jamie musing to
herself *Now this is happening, now that too has happened*
when she thought of him as she wandered a world of
long-unused, overgrown roads and narrow trails leading
to the reservoir's edge, searched for a granite outcrop, or
meandered directionless above Margaret's, the dog on
her heels, Jamie always walking, on the move, as if
motion and motion alone was any reason for living, as if
motion was the same as life. Keeping from Galen—as
she had kept from Damon—what she sometimes felt
when Damon brushed past her or closed in on her when
drunk, she electric in his wake, her body rearranging her
senses as though she were suffering from some molec-
ular near-collision, keeping from Galen—as she had
kept from Damon—what it had meant that first time in
his bed, Damon slow with drink and Jamie slowly
becoming erased, losing herself and then being only

herself and more incomprehensibly solitary than ever, awake and alone and aware of her loneliness despite of, because of, Damon asleep beside her, Damon who became with each trespass more a stranger than he had ever been in the beginning, and Jamie with each trespass becoming more removed from him than he would ever know; guarding within her too these trespasses.

Then tell me about yourself.

There's nothing to tell, she said again. And then looked at him, so gravely that he found her beauty painful to behold, and he palmed the floor and pushed himself away from her, so that he would not, could not, reach for her. He felt unmoored and imprisoned at the same instant, and rueful—because certain things were settled, he would leave, she would vanish more quickly than it ever took for Margaret's shutter to click, freeze some infinitesimal unit of time—and he felt rancor too, thinking she had misunderstood him, misread his reason for backing away, out of reach.

Listen, he began to explain, I don't give a damn about Damon. It's you—

Galen.

He stopped. The firelight flickered on her face, in her eyes, and she hesitated, thought: *I could, should, go with him, be with him, let this happen too.* But she sensed how unfair that would be, knew that whatever happened between them would never be—for him, perhaps even for her—just something that happened, despite the fact that it would happen only for a matter of time. She wanted nothing more than to confirm that she had no reason to stay, then walk away from a place she had once and would again consider just a stop along her way.

I know it's not Damon, she told him. And it's not you. It's me.

How old are you?

Seventeen.

Good lord, he exhaled. And at the thought of her on her own shook his head, said again: Come with me.

You have a life, Galen.

Not much of one.

It'd be worse, she told him, with me.

⌁

Galen drifted now and then into the sleep his mind would hardly allow, and each time he slipped under, cell walls closed in on him until his body jerked, jumpcut-hurtled him into wakefulness to escape their final crush. He finally gave up, sat up, contemplated the fire he occasionally stoked.

Just before daybreak Galen damped the embers, checked the shuttered windows, waited. After dawn, he heard the county plowtruck reach the top of the lane, and then he waited again, for Harlan's pickup to pull into the drive. When it did, Galen listened for the dog upstairs, whose muzzle was cupped in her hands—it did not make a sound—and heard Harlan pull the handbrake after he finished plowing, leave the engine running, open the pickup's door. He got out and walked about, looking, Galen knew, for a sign, any sign that she and the dog or the boy might be here; and then he heard Harlan slam the door shut, wind back down the drive, leave.

Jamie found Galen's note in the kitchen, one corner carefully tucked under the sugar jar, along with a worn ten-dollar bill. *The snowshoes were for you anyway* was written at the top of the hand-drawn map—of mountains, streams, ridges, landmarks—traversed by a trail of arrows leading from a box marked *Margaret's* to an *X*. Beside the *X*, Galen had written: *The merry-go-round. In case you change your mind.*

Twelve

The postmaster stared out over the season's shabbiness, the snowbanks already splattered by passing salt-encrusted cars, the roads at The Four Corners grungy with slush the consistency of sludge, the drab woods leafless, sepia-hued. When he saw Jamie coming toward the intersection, heading his way, he left the doorway and went back behind the counter, checked that the shoebox was where he'd left it.

He'd found the box among many others in his attic, stuffed with things long unused and long ago useless— a wreath crumbled almost to dust, a pair of children's shoes cast in bronze, his grammar-school diploma, bowties, motheaten suits, mothballs, cobalt elixir bottles, a Brownie camera—and things that weren't even his, undeliverable and unclaimed postcards from Ireland and France and Algeria and Greece and other faraway places

sent from phantom people to phantom addresses, squir-
reled away by him during his early years at that post
office in the city, or at least what passed for a city, a place
that had had at least some residents with the presence of
mind and heavy enough pocketbooks to travel farther
than the people in Dyers Corner or any of the upriver
milltowns ever considered. For in this place, most
people regarded vacation to mean the one or two weeks
a year they got paid to do whatever it was they'd been
waiting to do or finish the whole year long; and once
they did or finished that, they maybe weekended at a
seedy motel resort (if the cabins had kitchens), or took
a long drive and visited relatives, or got on a bus and
traveled somewhere but never went as far away as the
ocean (three hours by Greyhound), never mind to foreign countries they considered they had no business in
anyway, unless there was a war to fight. And given the
last war—which, the postmaster and at least some of his
fellow citizens noticed, four presidents not to mention
Congress never even bothered declaring, and the gen-
erals who sent troops to die there never bothered
explaining how they thought they might win without
having so much as a territorial objective in mind—most
people in Dyers Corner and the upriver towns figured
that they probably didn't have any business going to, vis-
iting, foreign countries even if there was a war to fight.

Especially given the way their sons had returned from Vietnam, some in coffins and others in wheelchairs and some whole, not a few with mohawks and a few with sniper skills and many with a faraway look in their eyes and some with nightmares, zero tolerance for loud noises, and a vitriolic contempt for what seemed to be half of their own generation, the half in the streets protesting the war who for the most part considered those veterans not as heroes and not even as patriots but as embarrassments, lunatics, murderers.

The postmaster had sifted through the boxes, looking for that shoebox, gone through all those useless things he piled about him on the dusty attic floor. He looked around just before he opened the shoebox's lid, bitterly realized: *This mess is the sum of my entire life.* And then he opened the box, found scores of black-and-white snapshots—only slightly curled, still glossy, their edges perfectly crimped. Some photographs were of friends after their factory shift, sternfaced young men and women solemn before a mill entrance; some of friends celebrating the Fourth of July with their children seated at picnic tables, the children's eyes too large for their faces; some of women he no longer recognized on their way somewhere, one wearing a dark blouse with a crocheted collar as fine as lace; and there was a portrait of his cousin Justine, in three-quarter profile with sallow

skin and dark eyes and darker mouth, her features
reminding him of gypsy bloodlines he'd glimpsed in
postcards from other worlds, postcards of barefoot, col-
orfully dressed women he once imagined dancing, arms
extended, on desert edges that gave way to flamingo-
filled lagoons. There were other photographs too—the
ones he wanted—in which he appeared, rakish and in
brogans and wearing a hat, his eyes always shadowed by
a brim, as well as notes and letters (from people almost
disremembered, most of them long ago dead) and a
faded blue hair ribbon that belonged to no one he could
recall. He did not reread the letters, fingered and discarded the ribbon, arranged the photographs he wanted
to give to the granddaughter of the only woman he had
ever loved—a love not forgotten but one he had considered no longer painful, at least until he was confronted
by all the sadness of his unspoken and unrequited passion in the person of Jamie Hall—and left the letters by
the discarded ribbon, left the opened boxes with their
contents disarrayed on the floor, brought the shoebox
with those chosen mementos to the post office and put
it on a shelf, waited for this moment.

Jamie came through the door and stamped her feet,
went to her empty box, unlocked it and took one step
back, forward, then closed and locked it. A pain shot
through the postmaster's chest, his arm, that made him

catch his breath. Is the mail in? she asked as he put the shoebox on the counter, brought his hands to rest on its lid.

It is, he said. And without knowing why, told her: Sorry.

He opened the shoebox. The topmost photograph was of him and his fellow workers in the dead of winter, on the reservoir, the iceblocks carved and stacked behind them and in the background a horse standing patient before its laden sled, beyond the horse and that sled the lake's open waters. He picked it up by a corner, examined it, cleared his throat and said: However, I have something for you.

But she was already gone, already beyond the door that was swinging shut, had already stepped into that shabby season and was gliding away from him, gliding through it, walking exactly in the same manner and with the same grace as her grandmother; and the postmaster blinked several times before he placed the snapshots back into the box, put the lid on—his hands not fluttering but trembling, his lower lip trembling too—and slid the shoebox onto the shelf. He had a lump in his throat, and his breath came hard, unevenly, as though he was in a boxing ring and being pummeled, and his eyes burned. There was, the postmaster told himself, no reason to feel humiliated, heartbroken. And he did not go to the doorway again: he denied himself that, for he knew—told himself—there was no reason, none at all, to stand there.

↪

Tsk, tsk, the pockmarked cashier hissed when Jamie walked into the convenience store, but Jamie ignored the woman's disapproval, asked for change of the ten-dollar bill, went to the telephone. She dialed Margaret's number, got the operator, deposited the requested amount.

Margaret? Jamie asked, hesitant, for the voice on the other end was not Margaret's. Margaret Horan, please.

Who's calling?

Jamie Hall.

I'm afraid I don't know you, the woman said.

I'm Margaret's housekeeper, upstate. I'm calling long distance. Is Margaret there?

Is anything wrong?

No. No, but I need to speak to Margaret, please.

Well, that won't be possible, the voice told her. Margaret has passed away.

Oh no, Jamie said, her knees giving, the receiver slipping from her hand. *Oh no*, she said again when she caught it up, steadied her legs, brought the receiver back to her ear.

I'm sorry to have given you a shock, the voice on the other end said, but it wasn't unexpected—I mean, Margaret was in her eighties—and it was all very fast, an aneurysm, a coma. She went very peacefully, about a month ago. More than that, actually. I should have had the phone disconnected but I haven't, I mean you can't imagine the mess here, I've no idea where to begin. Perhaps I should call the library to take all her books. Do you think they'd come to get them?

Excuse me?

Do you think the library would come for her books?

I—I really don't know.

Are there more books in the house there?

In the house? No.

What a relief. I haven't been up there in years. I remember it as being rather empty, not that I could tell you when I last saw the place. Is it?

Sorry?

Is the house empty? And by the way, could you speak a little louder?

Yes, Jamie said, raising her voice slightly. No, the house isn't empty.

What's in there?

Well, photographs. And furniture, dishes, rugs—*things*. Margaret used the house.

But are there any books?

Not really. A few, at the most.

Thank goodness. My aunt never said much about the house, and to tell you the truth we weren't close at all. Actually, she downright avoided the family for the most part. And got away with it because she was, as they always said, an *artiste*. Whatever that's supposed to mean, or justify.

Jamie could think of nothing to say. The operator broke in and asked for more coins, and Jamie deposited them. I hope you're not a live-in, Margaret's niece went on. I mean, you don't live in the house, do you?

No.

Well, that's a relief.

What should I do? Jamie asked.

About what?

Jamie closed her eyes, opened them. About the house.

I don't know—oh, I just hate tying up all these loose ends. It's all so complicated. I guess the best thing would be to lock up the house and drop the key in the mail— address it to Margaret, send it here, I mean, it's the strangest thing how the mail just keeps coming, bills and whatnot. Could you do that?

Jamie stared at the smudges around the phone's coin slot, wiped at them with her jacket sleeve. Not today, she said. And hung up. The cashier glared at her, folded her arms, clucked. No check, no credit, she said as Jamie walked past with tears welling in eyes, moved into the blurry aisles.

The cashier rung up the dogfood Jamie brought to the checkout, ignored her red-rimmed eyes, looked dourly at Jamie's knapsack. I'm not packing those cans if you're just going to unbag them and put them in that thing, she said.

↫

The snow on the reservoir was uneven, and here and there bald patches of ice shone slategray; toward the lake's middle, fingers of open water rippled darkly. Jamie numbly traversed the causeway, unaware of the knapsack eating into her shoulders, not bothering to hunch into the sharp windgusts that blew spindrift low across the reservoir, the road, as she made her way through the winter's unbroken dreariness, knowing that the only thing she could do now was what she had done when her mother died, leave everything as the dead would have wanted: the floors scrubbed and waxed, the furniture dusted and polished, the bathroom and kitchen spotless, the refrigerator emptied and unplugged and wide open, the windows shut, the closets neat, the door locked. As her mother lay dying—twenty-three days it took, once the cancer that had slowly gnawed

away at her for more than a year voraciously, swiftly ate
into her liver—solitude became Jamie's familiar, disbelief her only mooring. Until her mother's death-rattle
began—which Jamie was unprepared to witness, to
hear, for her mother did not go easily—and ended in a
final exhalation, that last breath, taking with it if the
poets are to be believed whatever soul her mother had,
Jamie had remained incredulous, unconvinced that her
mother would die. Then her mother turned ashen,
blued, grew cold; and her flesh—not yet rigid, not as it
would be in the funeral parlor, as ungiving as con-
crete—lost its resilience, so that when Jamie was finally
persuaded to leave her mother's bedside, after they
finally pried her fingers loose, her mother's lifeless hand
bore their impression.

The hospital social worker insisted that Jamie
become the state's ward no later than two days after her
mother was buried; and so, after the first shovel of earth
thudded onto the coffin, Jamie went back to the apartment—already in perfect order, spotless—and put the
knapsack on her back, the dog on a leash, locked the
door behind her and put the key in an envelope and left
that taped to the outside, slipped away from everything
and everyone she'd ever known. She carried in one
pocket what was left, after the funeral expenses, of the
small amount of money that could hardly be called their

lifesavings and yet was nothing but; and she left for the only other place she had ever been to, without knowing whether she'd ever come across a granite outcrop on the reservoir's edge or whether Dyers Corner would be smaller and maybe even meaner than the only town Jamie had ever lived in. She thought that people everywhere might be much like those she was leaving behind, stubbornly unwilling or simply too unwitting to know they were wretched, somewhat stupefied by the humdrum paucity of everyday life; people who found each day full of myriad meaningless choices—as to how to make ends meet, get by, get ahead, what to covet and what to wish for having been insidiously drummed into them as part of the catch-as-catch-can American dream—and just another day to get through. Jamie also considered that no one in Dyers Corner would know her, that people would hardly notice her, and that from there she'd move on, to anywhere. Instead, she found herself with a roof over her head, near the reservoir, and gave herself over to coincidence, inertia, Damon's astounding hands. Thinking the while that she was growing up, and that by doing so she might outgrow her grief.

Margaret, she reflected, is dead somewhere.

Margaret, she reflected, is in a hole somewhere, where she shouldn't be. For Margaret had wanted to be buried in the orchard—she hadn't even wanted a rough-

hewn pinewood coffin, said that a sheet would do and
that if she were just wrapped in one then the grave could
be shallow, which meant the digging would inconven-
ience no one—but she was unable to get the legal permit
now required to be laid to rest on her own property. Not
that the dead care where they're dumped, Margaret had
told Jamie, but that sheet matters to me, and there's not
a cemetery on this continent that doesn't demand a box.
Which might suit me fine if there were cardboard ones
on offer, but there aren't. Watching Jamie's reaction with
those appraising, intelligent eyes, laughing at her
momentary astonishment that anyone would even
dream of a cardboard casket.

Jamie's mother, Margaret: gone, dead, Jamie told
herself, could hear Margaret say and from them there's
no judgment; and she pushed on through the increas-
ingly bitter blow, the ill-fitting boots chafing. Where the
road forked she considered pressing on to Margaret's
without stopping, hesitated, and without knowing why
took the turn toward Damon's instead. Outside the
house a stationwagon she did not recognize was parked,
its reardoor open, boxes piled within; and she hesitated
again, then went on anyway, skirting the car and
crossing the yard, trying the door. She let herself in.
Chairs and the armchairs and the kitchen table, a mattress and nightstand were pushed against one side of the

room like uneven ship ballast, and in a far corner the coils of an electric heater glared orange. The faucet still dripped.

Damon came down the stairs, peering over the edge of the box he carried, and started as though he'd seen an apparition. He recovered, dropped the box on the floor, watched Jamie walk over to an electric heater he'd placed in an empty corner, peel the knapsack from her shoulders, let it fall to the floor. When she turned and faced him, she felt the heat upon her calves, put her hands in her pockets.

Well, well, Damon said, what have we here.

What have we here.

She had no answer to that, could say nothing in response, said instead: You're moving out.

Damon studied her for a moment, reached into an inner pocket, brought out a flask, uncapped the whiskey, offered it to her. She declined with a shake of her head. He took a drink, grimaced, took another drink, let the liquor brace him.

My wife's pregnant, he said.

Something unraveled inside her and Jamie wobbled, felt the earth's axis shift an infinitesimal iota, thought she might lose her balance, she who had fallen time and again into Damon's hands and into his body and was now falling into nothingness as though being spun into some great void. She took a deep breath, fought the reel, thought: And now the end, now an ending, now this has happened too.

Congratulations, she told him.

You don't mean that.

I think it's what I'm supposed to say.

Yeah, well. So, anyway, I'm becoming a father, packing it in. I'm a changed man.

Liar: the word came to her, but she did not say it. She watched him bring the flask to his mouth. You seem the same, she told him.

Don't deceive yourself, he replied, taking a sip.

She stepped away from the heater, picked up the knapsack, shouldered it.

Whoa, Damon said as she made for the door, catching her by a jacket sleeve, holding fast. Whoa, he said again as she pulled away from him, not so fast.

Let go, she told him.

Uh-uh. Not till you tell me why you came back.

I'm not back.

Hell you're not. So maybe stay a while, for old times' sake.

Jamie tussled free of him, slammed the door behind her. He followed, paused at the door and put his forehead against it, squeezed his eyes shut and silently cursed himself, then reached for the handle and opened the door, called out her name. By the time he put on his jacket and went to the car, she was already at the turn onto the reservoir road. He closed the stationwagon's reardoor, got in, put the flask on the dashboard, turned the engine over, rolled down the passenger window, caught up to her. She wouldn't look at him, or stop. He slowed, drove beside her.

Leave me alone, she finally told him.

You going to Margaret's?

None of your business.

Let me give you a lift. I'm sorry. Really, I'm sorry. I am. For god's sake, Jamie—

She got in. Margaret's, he said, and she nodded. The car listed slightly, the heater blew cold. She watched the winter landscape bleed into the solemn winter sky and said not a word. The boxes shifted when they turned off the reservoir road, slipped backward as they climbed upward along the lane. Damon drove without speaking until they reached the sumacs at the edge of Margaret's drive, where he braked, whistled low.

Margaret's paying someone to plow?

Margaret, she thought, is a ghost.

He let the car idle, looked at Jamie's chiseled profile, flawless skin, her windtangled hair, regretted that his best years were behind him. He reached for the flask, uncapped it.

No, she said then. Someone just plows it.

Someone?

A poacher.

Damon took a swig. Well, he told her, you'll do all right for yourself. Trappers, poachers.

She got out of the car with her knapsack, began to close the door, thought better of it, leaned in. You haven't changed a bit, she told him. And with that slammed the door and walked away, heard him turn the car around and leave, fought back a humiliation she had never known, a loneliness she knew all too well, an exhaustion she had no strength left to battle. When she opened Margaret's door, she fell to her knees, hugged the dog, sobbed at the shock of such unmediated and irremediable sadness coursing through her, the painful realization that so much love within her had already been thwarted and might remain so forever.

⤻

Jamie stayed that night, the next, not knowing whether she imagined Margaret's presence or was privy to such, dreamed of Margaret and of her mother and of the boy in what sleep overcame her in the armchair or on the rug before the late-night blazes she allowed herself. She could do little except bide and abide time, which pressed upon her with the force of gravity, omnipresent and holding her within a stasis to which she seemed rooted, though she was rootless, homeless. She walked with the dog on a leash, disallowed it its freedom, kept to the lane, afraid that its tracks or her footprints in the orchard, anywhere, might signal their presence to Harlan, if he arrived before the next snow. She was also afraid that if she didn't walk the dog on the leash it might vanish, as had everything, everyone else, she had ever loved. She cocooned herself within the house, straightened closets and cupboards, swept and mopped and waxed and dusted, in the end cleaned the refrigerator and unplugged it, saw to it that everything was in its place. Except the snowshoes. Which did not belong at Margaret's or to her, and which she could not leave behind, which she would return to Galen. To whom she would tell the news of Margaret's death, then be on her way.

She waited for the inevitable, for the snow that would cover all traces of their leaving. The morning it began, she rose before dawn and checked the darkness of the world, made coffee, grimly awaited the day. At first light she fed the dog, washed and dried and put away the cup, the bowl, gathered the cold ashes from the fireplace into the throw she had used to carry kindling, folded it carefully so that no ashes would spill. Then stepped outside into winter's gray shimmer and, cradling the bundle and with the unleashed dog at her side, made her way to the orchard.

Somewhere within it, perhaps close to where one of Margaret's grandchildren was buried and maybe even on the same spot Margaret had stood when she burned the flag that had covered her other grandchild's coffin, Jamie scattered the throw's contents as if performing an age-old ritual—dust to dust, ashes to ashes—the small pieces of charcoal rolling away and looking much like bits of charred bone, the lighter ashes settling, almost immediately disappearing beneath a layer of crystalline snowbeads. She shook out the throw one last time, surveyed all about her as if memorizing the lay of the land, took in the crabapple trees in the freeze, the snowpack undulating over the uneven earth, the sumacs with their tufted rustblood plumes dusted with icy drizzle, the mountains in part obscured by the precipitation, and then she folded the throw and walked back toward the house, which she saw as if for the first time, rambling and desolate and improbable at the end of a lane leading nowhere else. She left the dog outside and checked each room one last time, shuttered windows, extinguished lamps. She turned the thermostat down to its lowest setting, brought the snowshoes and her knapsack onto the porch, locked the door and put the key on the jamb above, tucked her jeans into her socks, tightened her boot laces, straightened.

The dog was nowhere in sight.

She whistled, waited, whistled again. She fought back her fear, listened to the drizzle hit with a sizzling sound, strained to hear anything else, whistled again. And then she heard, as if from a great distance, the dog yelping in pure canine panic, and her blood ran cold and she yelled the dog's name and then heard the dog more clearly, saw it struggle over the orchard wall in panic, yelping still, and flounder toward her with something twisted around its neck, its chest, one leg. When it reached her she fumbled to free the dog of the harness, the dog hardly standing still, panicking, whining the while, until she finally got it off. And then the dog sat down, raised its muzzle, howled deep and long and woeful.

She dropped the harness in the drive, got the knapsack on, stepped into the snowshoes and with trembling hands did the bindings, the dog licking at her face, and when she thought they were strapped to her boots as tightly as possible she shooed the dog in front of her and at the top of the drive stepped into Galen's wake, made her way toward the pumphouse, shuffling, unable to match Galen's stride, the snowshoes' tips catching in his steps. When she realized she needed to walk on top of the snow beside his tracks, no matter how cumbersome the snowshoes seemed, no matter how unsure she was to walk in them, she pushed on beyond the pumphouse and settled into a resolute pace. The dog leading.

She did not look back, as she was afraid. She did not know who had thrown that harness on the dog, or why, and until she convinced herself that no one was following them—could, would, follow, for the going was hard, and the way, perhaps, she told herself, long, the weather certain to worsen—she did not so much as glance over her shoulder. When she finally did, there was no one, nothing, and she went on, not understanding the boy's madness, unaware that Harlan would, that afternoon, plow into Margaret's drive and uncover the harness, cut the pickup's engine and get out, walk to the drive's topmost end and follow her trail past the pumphouse and upward along the stream, curse when he came across another set of human tracks, which belonged to the boy. These would send Harlan back to the pickup for his hat, gloves, rifle, cartridges, make him calculate the little daylight left to him and inwardly rage because of how far ahead of him the girl, the boy, the dog must be. And then set out after them.

Thirteen

The boy did not think in terms of life and death, for though he could distinguish in some way between the two he had no concept of their difference except as a matter of stillness and that as a matter of degree. And so he did not know whether the child he dragged by its harness into the timelessness of day and night had simply quieted and lived or simply died and quieted, for the boy was mindful only of his sibling's weight and of the going and of nothing besides. He wandered tirelessly and sometimes in circles and settled nowhere for more than a few hours at a time until after he broke out onto the ice-encrusted reservoir edge where the snow was somehow less, and he walked twisted and crablike upon it, with one arm crooked before him and one arm flung behind and pulling, the child facedown and plowing and the boy making his way slowly toward the line of bobhouses perched along a low, salient promontory and standing out blackly in the waning light. He did not release the child even after reaching these, but pulled it from one bobhouse to another, kicking at the rusted locks on rotted, ill-fitting doors, breaking in. He found in one a tin of crackers and in another a filled kerosene lamp and in another two cans of beans, and with the unlit lamp in his free hand and the tin and cans in the fowlsack he finally shoved his burden into a bobhouse and left it, went back and ran amok, within the other bobhouses flinging fishhooks everywhere, snarling and snapping fishing lines, smashing ice skimmers on the floors until they bent, trampling fishtraps underfoot. When he wreaked what havoc that occurred to him he went back to the bobhouse where his sibling lay motionless on the floor. He searched his pockets for the lighter and lit the oil lamp, closed the door, set the prone child over the fishing hole, opened the crackers and ate ravenously, knifed open a can of beans and chipped at the frozen mess, melting in his mouth the bits he managed to dig out. Later, he worked at getting the harness off the child, whose limbs had stiffened and were so ungiving that only after the boy snapped one of its arms under his weight was he able to pull the harness free. He looped the tether and harness together and put it into the fowlsack, then lay on the floor beside his sibling and gazed at

the child's face, for in the flickering play of light, decep-
tive shadows gave to its half-closed eyes some semblance
of expression, though the dark pupils were wide and
unseeing. The boy remained still for a long time, then
rose and got a cracker and thrust it into the child's rigid,
unclosed mouth, but the child did not move, did not
chew; and the next thing the boy knew, light was seeping
into the bobhouse through the cracks in its planking. He
lay for some time as if in a dreamless void, then rolled
onto his belly, gathered himself onto all fours and
stretched his backend into the air, barked small, almost
soundless barks that were less than canine, much less
than human. When he got to his feet he stood over the
quiescent child with the cracker in its mouth, toed the
child's torso and then stepped on it, waited for motion
or a cry and then waited for neither.

When he woke again, the light of the day was the
light of all days and any day and so indistinct that the
boy did not know whether it was dawn or dusk. He put
his back against a wall and took up the knife, pried open
the other can of beans, and was so startled when a bubbling noise ripped from the child that he dropped the
can and caught at it in midair, its lid slicing open the
base of his thumb to the bone and cutting deep into his
palm. The boy howled as he watched his blood spurt,
screamed until it slowed, and then he cowered, backed

away from his sibling, fearful that it would make another explosive sound and hearing only and for a very long while: *drip. drip. drip. drip.* The boy began to know pain as he had never known it before, something constant unlike the rain of blows and fiercer, and he sucked at the wound and tried to push its split sides together, later pressed it against his jacket. He moaned at the pain, sometimes slept, sometimes woke. When he could not sleep at all he kicked at the child's torso, its limbs, and when it made no sound he finally touched it, tearing the filthy, half-frozen shirt from its body and wrapping this about his hand as tightly as he could before once again reaching for the can, wrenching its lid back, digging out small hunks of frozen beans and stuffing them into his mouth.

He whimpered the while, but his sibling was silent, remained silent even when the boy threw the empty can against the wall, even when he pushed the child head-first into the hole cut in the bobhouse floor. With the harness in the fowlsack and the sack on his shoulder, with the earflap hat falling into his eyes and his hand ludicrously bandaged, he made his way to where he knew the dog was; and through the silver drizzle he watched the dog nose the snow's surface as she scattered ashes in the orchard, the boy wondering at nothing and crouching impassively but for plunging his wounded hand deep into the snow, the freeze numbing the pain but not dissipating the fever already rising within him. He stayed there until she turned and went back to the house, until the dog came to him, and then he tumbled through the snow back the way he came, falling and rolling about, flailing his arms to make the creature leap around him, leading it away from the house. After taking the harness out of the fowlsack he threw himself onto his back and waited for the dog to stand over him, sniff and lick him, before grabbing the creature and wrestling it onto its side and straddling it. He put the tether between his teeth and managed to get the harness half on, but the dog panicked, thrashed, yelped, struggled to get away, the cloth unraveling about the boy's hand and the wound gushing again. And then the dog was gone, half-yoked and gone, disappeared into the snowfall. The taste of leather in the boy's mouth bitter.

Fourteen

Jamie stopped at an abandoned quarry that broke the forested monotony of the mountainside, its massive length scablike and jagged as an old wound unhealed upon the earth. Unhealed and unhealing, for not bush nor tree nor brush had taken root in that jumble of stone and pit and tailing piles beneath the smoothed, worked ledges that rose and jutted dark and evenly through the snowfall, fanging long icicles. The going was rough, her ankles rubbed raw, the snowshoes so cumbersome that she at one point took them off only to sink to her knees in the snow and exhaust herself by trying to push on without them. And then she strapped them on again, went on following Galen's trail. Which was filling with a fine thin snow that came down heavily now, heavier than she'd ever known any drizzle to fall, and though she was loath to pause—afraid she might lose Galen's trail by day's end, if it took so long, fearing too that his trail might go on for days—she needed to catch her breath, rest. She walked to the ledge and broke off a long icicle to suck, for the snow she had eaten along the way did nothing to quench her thirst. She put a piece of ice in her mouth, looked back for the first time, saw the old quarry road whiteslash a long contour behind her, was awed by how Galen had always appeared or disappeared by that pumphouse at any time of day as though he were only a stroll away. Which he was not.

Neither Galen nor Margaret had ever mentioned how far away, or where, Galen lived. Margaret told Jamie only that Galen was a man who, for reasons she would not go into, was determined to be isolate and self-sufficient, as if—Margaret had added—Galen had never heard that men are not islands and as if he had no understanding that what makes human beings fully and not partially human is their commonality, their notion of and faith in a common weal. Self-sufficiency is such a ludicrous idea, Margaret—not disparaging, only mildly exasperated—went on, you'd think we were beyond that but we're not; and Galen might have his reasons and they might even be good reasons but they're not good enough even though they're probably a hell of a lot more to the point than what other people use as an excuse to live that way: individualism. Rugged or otherwise. The problem with this country—Margaret had shaken her head then, waved expansively at the orchard, forest, mountains—is its hinterland, or no, the problem with the hinterland is this country, and the notion that its greatness all comes down to each and every one of us being uniquely free. Except that it's hard to square the freedom of the individual with a country that's never been very good at putting up with differences or being sympathetic to any form of patriotism that doesn't have to do with paying the mortgage or rent and owning things and wanting to own more things. You see, Margaret told Jamie, the truth about America is that individualism is barely tolerated, unless it means conformity or except when it masquerades as self-sufficiency. One for all and all for one, but every man for himself. And so Galen chose, no—Margaret corrected herself—thinks he was forced to choose, had only one choice. Though I'd say he knows better.

Than what? Jamie had asked, Margaret glimpsing in her for the first time a curiosity Jamie quickly disguised by nonchalantly pushing a strand of hair behind her ear and looking over to where the dog was sprawled in the orchard's shade.

Than to go it alone, Margaret said.

Jamie wondered now whether what Margaret had termed Galen's isolate self-sufficiency might not have everything to do with the simple fact that being alone was the best way to shield yourself from harm and hurt, the world being—or so Jamie thought she had learned in little time—a more or less inhospitable place, the people within it mostly mean or unkind or untrustworthy or unconcerned or indifferent, or if they weren't, were in the end (like her mother, her father, Margaret, Damon) just dead or as good as dead. And she wondered too whether she'd made such a choice, or would. For it seemed to her she'd had no choice but to walk away from her mother's grave, away from her hometown; and yet she had chosen, to head for Dyers Corner and the reservoir and maybe a granite outcrop before moving on, and then she had chosen to stay only to find that she had no choice but to leave. And she'd failed somewhere along the way, she thought, not excusably but unmistakably and very miserably, as proven by the fact that here she was, in the middle of nowhere and in the dead of winter, no road in sight and with less on her back than she'd once carried, and with nothing in her pockets. At least, Jamie consoled herself, she happened to be standing, walking, on her own two feet, not that there was any choice involved. She broke off another piece of ice, the snow biting at her face, and shivered, the film of sweat on her skin already clammy, cold, looked down at the snowshoes and almost jumped out of them when the dog lunged past her with a fierce growl.

The boy was small in the distance, diminished by the landscape and obscured by the snow, and though Jamie could not distinguish the angle of his skewed hat or the odd crook to one arm or see his wrapped hand, his bloodless gaze, she knew he was faltering in the snow's depth. The dog moved menacingly toward the boy, growling still, hackles up. *Come,* she cried, dropping the icicle, concentrating on skimming the surface of the snow, on speed, on getting away from the boy, for the dog would follow her, she knew, the dog would chase after her. And then the boy bayed, a sound that set her teeth on edge and stopped her in her tracks, made her look back to see the dog racing toward her and the boy motionless, down, sitting in the snow. He continued to bay, yowl: Jamie heard him long after she and the dog passed the end of the quarry, where there was no road and only the forest, pushed on in what she thought was Galen's trail until she was no longer sure. When she couldn't hear the boy anymore, she no longer knew whether she and the dog were following anything but a deer trail, and without stopping she pulled out Galen's curious, hand-drawn map, looked around, saw nothing but woods and somewhere beyond the treetops the sky that poured down. Behind her, her own trail led back to the quarry, to the boy who—and this she could not know—still sat there, his wounded hand thrust in the

snow and his mouth skewed open, watching the mountains above him claw at the sky.

⤳

The wind rose and soughed through the sprucetops
that Jamie could barely see, which remained unrevealed
to her because of those thickly intertwined lower
boughs that blotted out the snow as well and enshad-
owed all. The dog slowed, and she waited for it to lead
the way; for though she did not know whether it had
picked up Galen's scent any more than she could fathom
how much distance they still had to cover, she had
nothing else to go on. The ground beneath the trees was
almost snowless, and for a while Jamie carried the snowshoes and walked on solid earth, surprised by her sense
of weightlessness and the joy of unencumbered motion
despite her sore ankles. When the spruces thinned, she
strapped the snowshoes back on and determinedly
regained her stride, followed the dog, noticed little of
the world she passed through except its seeming end-
lessness.

And so she did not see the hunter. He stood poised,
riflebutt nestled in his shoulder's hollow and barrel
resting on top of the blind, listening to the thrash within
the forest. He cocked the hammer, muffling its sound
with his thumb, shifted ever so slightly, tried to antici-

pate what might materialize and was sure that not even a bear pulled from hibernation by starvation would be so heedless. He steadied himself, a forefinger resting on the trigger, the cold of the barrel distinct in his hand, waited. When the dog and girl moved into the sights it was his breath that exploded in a cloud of white as he jerked the rifle upward. He swore vociferously under his breath, the adrenaline coursing through him, his chest going wet with sweat, at the same moment the dog shied, leaped sideways and back at the same moment she saw the hunter and stopped, a gasp escaping her.

I swear, the hunter called out, I just hate surprises in the woods.

Jamie reached for the dog.

No harm done, and for that I'm right thankful, he continued, touching his hand to his hat. Some people will shoot at anything they hear before seeing what it is they're aiming at. I stopped doing that years ago, after I killed a dog by accident. It near broke my heart. I keep dogs myself. The only naturally good animal in the world, wouldn't you say?

Jamie nodded.

Is that dog friendly?

She nodded again, said: Yes.

Well, come on, then, there's no sense in just standing there. That's a fine-looking creature. Part wolf, if I'm not mistaken. Or maybe one of them Alaskan dogs.

Part something, Jamie said, coming toward him. He turned so that the scar that began below one cheekbone and coursed purplish the length of his face, his neck, might not deter her, might remain unseen.

You should put a red bandana around that dog's neck. You should be wearing red yourself. I mean, it's hard enough for a body in the woods to tell what's coming at him unless it's wearing a color animals don't bother with.

The dog sniffed the hunter's boots, his hand, wagged its tail.

Fine-looking dog, he said again, looking sideways at her, taking in the half-frozen, half-drenched scarf wrapped about her head and neck, her ice-matted hair, soaked shoulders, the too-thin jacket, the knapsack, the snowshoes.

You look like you could use something to warm you up, he remarked. I've got an old thermos here with some coffee still in it.

Thank you.

He stood the rifle against the blind, got the thermos, poured what was left into the thermos cap. She took the cup with both hands, thanked him again.

I take it you're not aiming to go a good deal further in this weather, he said.

I don't know.

You lost?

I don't know that either. I was following a trail and then I wasn't. I'm trying to get to an old animal farm.

You're not close, but not so far either. It's in that direction, he said, pointing. There's not much there, just a trapper. Friend of yours?

She nodded, tried not to stare at the scar, apparent now that the hunter looked straight at her, and then he averted his face again. Well, he said, I must say I never much liked trappers. That's not hunting. No sport to it, setting snares and laying bait and walking away, coming back to find some animal dead of bloodloss or shock if their neck's not broken or they got caught by a paw. I found a bobcat foot in a trap once, the cat gone. Gnawed off its own leg, chewed right through it. The worst thing about a trap, though, is that it'll snap shut at anything. Dog, person.

She looked at him over the rim of the thermos cap, said nothing.

I'm not saying your friend's not a decent sort, mind you. A bit queer, maybe, something of a loner. Not that it matters. And he gave me a hand recently, helped me haul a deer out past his property, didn't want a thing for his time and effort. I gave him a good cut of hind anyway. One kindness deserves another.

She crouched in the snowshoes, wiped out the

thermos cap with a handful of snow, straightened, handed it to the hunter.

So, how far have you come? he asked.

Pretty far. How far do I have left to go?

Well, you just keep heading that way in my tracks, and in about a half-hour's time you'll see a trail cut off to the left. The snowshoe tracks are covered, but they're there, depressed-like. Follow those. You'll get where you're going. And keep that dog close, you don't want it getting snared.

I'll do that. Thank you again for the coffee.

Don't think of it. By the way, did you see any deer along the way?

No, Jamie answered. She hesitated, then told him: But there was a boy.

A boy?

A ways back. At a quarry.

Was he hunting?

She shook her head.

Like I said, I truly hate surprises in the woods. It can scare the bejesus out of you. If he wasn't hunting, what was he doing?

The last time I saw, just standing there.

The hunter furrowed his brow, kept his face angled from her. Well, that doesn't make much sense. Then again, lots of things don't.

⤻

As the trees thinned and Jamie broke out from the forest and reached the edge of a great clearing, Harlan— nowhere near the quarry and having no knowledge that any such quarry had ever existed, as he was unfamiliar with the terrain that Galen knew intimately, could navigate in the blackest of moonless nights—gave in to the time and daylight left and to the ache in his knees. He hoisted the rifle he had carried with one hand onto his shoulder and turned back from his pursuit, retraced his steps, a solitary stalker perturbed and perturbing in the gathering dusk. He broke through the snow even when walking in her snowshoed tracks, cursed aloud each time he did, cursed her for having foiled him, cursed the boy because he had not caught up to him, cursed her dog because he hated dogs, cursed the weather, and cursed Galen—for lying, for throwing him off track, for protecting the girl. Who, Harlan promised himself, could no more be shielded now than the boy. Not by Galen, not by anybody.

Jamie crossed the clearing with difficulty, for the snow—no longer fine, but thick, wet—clung to the snowshoes, weighed them down. The dog struggled too, in the deep softness, here and there tiredly paused belly-deep before slow-bounding again through the white immensity that spilled from a tripe-textured sky. At the far edge of the clearing she came across poles leaning at odd angles, set at what had once been precise intervals, and where they pulled most downward she stepped over a tangle of what must have been the topmost fencing wire, crossed into what had once been pasture. She could barely discern Galen's trail, crested a gentle slope, then saw it: not Galen's wake but the carousel's peaked, circular roof, the slanted floor higher than the snow's depth, the wooden horses. And when she drew near she stopped, marveled at the arrested steeds despite their fading paint, admired their once fierce eyes flaking now like dried petals; stopped and then went on, past a maze of rundown stables and holding pens and sheds, past a miniature mill straddling a creek, the mill's roof pushing through the snow and the black-flowing creek narrowed by drifts, and then she stopped again, called out Galen's name. The dog went ahead as if knowing where to go, made its way to a cabin and climbed onto its porch, sniffed at a door and settled, leaning, panting, against it. She undid the snowshoes and stepped out of them at the porch's edge, stepped onto it, placed them against the wall, dropped her knapsack, knocked on the door, called Galen's name again.

The door did not give. She ran her hand over the top of its frame, hoping to find a key, found nothing, then cupped her hands against her face and peered into the windows on either side of the door, saw only dimness within. She began to shiver violently, did not know what to do, sat with her back against the wall in a posture of pure exhaustion, took the wet scarf from her head and pulled at the icicles in her hair, then got up and emptied the knapsack, took out the cans of frozen dogfood she had no opener for and what clothes she had, stripped off her jacket and sweater and soaked undershirt and pulled on everything she could, then got into the jacket once again and lay on her side beside the dog, felt the cold numb her. She awoke in the night, frozen and famished and too weak to do anything but place her hands under the dog; and sometime the next day the sun's wintry glare off the snow glowed red within her eyelids like a blank wall of blood.

Fifteen

Oh god, she heard Galen say. Jamie tried to rise but her head felt as if weighted with stone. She had no feeling in her hands and feet, was unable to open her eyes, heard a key turn in a latch, felt herself being lifted, carried, put on something soft, uneven. The dog, was all she managed to say. She felt a hand on her forehead, her throat, heard Galen's voice tell her: The dog's here. And then she understood that she was being buried under blankets, and slipped under, under.

Galen worked quickly, lit the woodstove, left the grate fully open so the fire would blaze, then lifted the end of the blankets and undid her boots, peeled off her socks, saw the raw wounds about her ankles, sat and held her bare feet one after the other between his hands to warm them. Her skin the color of alabaster, her eyelids and the circles beneath her eyes shading bluish. The dog nosed Jamie's elbow, but she did not stir. When the cabin had warmed and the circulation returned to her feet, Galen retrieved Jamie's knapsack and what clothes she'd stripped out of on the porch, took in the cans of frozen dogfood, stood the snowshoes against the far inner wall, gave the dog a half-loaf of bread and a tin of water, made yarrow tea with sugar and whiskey, roused her. Drink this, he said, propping her head with a pillow, holding the mug for her, and she opened her eyes and gazed at him feverishly, turned her head at the smell of the brew. He touched her paper-dry skin, felt the burn. I thought you'd never come, she rasped.

I could say the same for you.

Don't fall asleep yet, Galen told her when she closed her eyes after the second swallow. She came to again, struggled to sit up, fell back, said: Margaret died, oh Galen Margaret's dead. And then he knew, knew why she had come, knew too a loss that made him reel, catch his breath, left him unable to say anything but *shhhhhh*. Shhhhhh, he told her again, pulling her into a sitting position, Jamie feeling every bone, every cell in her body, as he stripped the sweaters and damp shirt from her, put her arms through the sleeves of one of his flannel shirts and then through a thick cardigan, lay her back down, put a pair of wool socks on her feet, tucked the blankets around her again.

She came in and out of consciousness, suffered tremors, lost days. Sometimes she heard him move quietly about the cabin; at other times the crackling of burning wood reverberated dully, painfully, through her; sometimes she felt the dog nose her hand, lick her fingers. Galen helped her to and from the bathroom when she managed to wake; he made broth from deer bones, tea infusions of slippery elm and wild sage, spoonfed her. Jamie would sometimes throw off the blanket, tear at her clothes clammy with sweat, sense Galen beside her, open her eyes and see no one at all; and at other times she sensed no one beside her only to find Galen there. She would look at him fixedly then, see him through some filmy thickness only the drowning are privileged to see at the last moment, try to concentrate, summon words, speak, then sleep again without knowing whether she'd woken at all. Sometimes the radio played quietly, or perhaps it was Galen who sang softly in an astoundingly sweet voice; she could not tell which and was not uncomforted.

Where were you? she once asked Galen or dreamed she asked him, and she thought he responded: Caching traps, camping out, and then she thought or dreamed of him coming in and out of hoary, humpbacked igloos beneath trees christmased with traps whose shapes took on the form of angels and stars drawn by children. Dyers

Corner, for supplies, is what he actually told her, the truth but not its entirety: for he had gone there in the hope that he might catch a glimpse of her, learn what had become of her. He spent the night on a bar's backroom floor, walked around the town in which it was impossible not to see every resident in the spate of some four morning or afternoon hours, and spent an afternoon, evening, and a morning there. He did not see her and learned nothing, bought staples, hitchhiked back, envisioning her and the dog in this harsh season making their way through it, heading somewhere, anywhere, away from him. Thinking of having missed her and ruing the faultlines of his life, which like unaccountable seismic quakes and with unnerving inevitability always shifted him, still shifted him, into the wrong place at the wrong time. If only, he'd told himself remorsefully. If only he'd run into her, could go wherever it was she was going. If only he had not gone with Harlan and Bobby's girl. If only he had not lost all those years.

If only she would stay, he told himself now. If only he could bear her leaving.

He watched over her. Jamie babbled feverishly in her sleep, awoke from nightmares half-aphasic. Galen could not understand what was real, what was unreal. She told him repeatedly that Margaret was dead, that her mother was dead, spoke to both Margaret and her mother from

time to time; and once, in the middle of a night, she
called out for the dog, then cried out in panic when
Galen woke her. She sobbed without crying, desperately
tried to get to her feet, fought Galen until he quieted her
by holding her close, enveloping her, touching his cheek
to her hair, waiting for the nightmare to recede. It was
just a bad dream, he repeated again and again. You're
awake now, it's over, you're awake.

A game of fetch, with bones not sticks. The dog dead,
and Galen murmuring, It's over. Tell me. Tell me about
it. But Jamie could not find the words to say A game of
fetch, with bones not sticks, the boy with a bag full of
bones, my mother's bones and Margaret's bones and Margaret's dead grandsons' bones, and I'm the dog or the dog
is me or the dog is just the dog and the boy is throwing
stickbones for me to chase but I can't get to them, can't
retrieve them because he throws them too far, no end to the
ice that isn't even solid but full of floes, and no matter how
far I run after the bones they float away though I turn
around to find the boy even closer than he was and
throwing another, then another, and then there you are, on
the ice and laughing but you're not standing, you're
crawling around and laughing, and your legbones are gone
and then I'm crawling too because the boy has my ribs or
maybe my shinbones in his hands, and now the dog isn't
me and I'm not the dog because the dog is part of the game,

the dog is playing fetch, jumping over us, until the boy throws a boomerang bone and the dog races to where the bone angles back in flight, and the dog leaps, slips, its backbone violently snapping to the sound of ice cracking and then the floes drift apart and the boy disappears, laughing, laughing.

Tell me, Galen said again.

The dog is dead.

The dog is here, Jamie, the dog is fine.

The dog died. The boy took our bones.

Shhhhhhhh.

He followed me.

You're here now.

He was at the quarry.

It's just a dream, Galen told her, rocking her, feeling the terrifying heat of her body. He held her for a long time, dozed, waked, extricated himself gently, covered her, stoked the woodstove before climbing into the loft and stretching out on the mattress to sleeplessly await a distant dawn.

Her fever did not break, though on the first fetid morning that winter erupted into thaw, she was cooler—warm, hot, but no longer burning—to the touch. Galen stepped into that false spring morning, studied the fog rising from the snow and the melt dripping from fantastic icicles on the ends of conifer branches, low-whistled to the dog, left the door to the cabin cracked open. He went to the shed where he pegged his pelts and checked their tautness, made adjustments, noticed the dog raise its nose to examine those cured pelts that hung from hooks, stand on its hind legs to nip at one, two; and Galen thought of pioneers trapped in deep winter, their food long gone and the skins their children sat on receding inch by inch as they cut off small pieces and singed the fur away and toasted what was left on paltry fires and chewed the strips listlessly, their tongues blackening from the soot and their teeth ground down to nubs, dying the while. Thought: how weak they must have been when false spring sprang, how deep the snow, how treacherous the season—treacherous here too, Galen knew, the thaw impermanent if enough to allow treesap to flow before winter once again congealed it, reclaimed all, froze the earth and covered it with sheets of sleet, endless snow again. There's time yet, he said to the dog, shooing it from the shed, the dog then following him to the woodpile. Galen chopped kindling first, splitting the softer wood, birch and pine, until his muscles warmed to the task, before working the aged ash and oak and hickory to fit the woodburning stove, using the back of his ax to split the pieces along frozen cracks and then swinging the blade into their long-grained meat. When he fin-

ished he carried the wood in and stacked it, saw that she
was awake and sitting up, taking in her surroundings: a
chair beside the woodstove and the stove's angled pipe,
the snowshoes against the wall, two trunks and a rolltop
oak desk, her jacket and clothes hung on pegs beside the
closet door, the table with its oilcloth cover and beyond
it the counter and cupboards, a small sideboard pushed
against the back wall, the bathroom door under the loft.

You're better, Galen said by way of greeting,
touching the back of his fingers to her forehead.

She nodded, tried to swallow. Her throat was tight,
sore.

I'll make coffee, he said. You can try to shower if
you're up for it.

She nodded again. Galen brought her another of his
shirts and a worn pair of jeans too large for her, a belt,
helped her to the bathroom, closed the door. She stood
in the small stall and let the water beat brutally against
her skin, leaned against the drywall, felt what strength
she had seep away. It seemed to her to take forever to
dress, towel her hair, open the door to see the percolater
and mugs on the table, bread toasting on the woodstove's top, Galen pouring coffee. Jamie crossed the
room, sat down, waved away the toast. I don't think I
can, she told him. From outside came the smell of
snowmelt, and fog wisped through the open door as the

dog shouldered its way in and padded over to her. She touched the creature's head, looked around.

It was the office, Galen said. Once upon a time.

And now? she asked hoarsely.

Now it's home. A makeshift one at that. It was a lot more cluttered before I built the loft. Colder, too, before it was insulated.

And the house?

There wasn't any. There was a platform, where we pitched the tent we lived in during the season. The rest of the year, we lived in town.

Dyers Corner?

Galen shook his head. Goffston. Away from the river, the reservoir, in the other direction. Two miles out the dirt drive, another twelve northwest on the road.

I feel lost, Jamie said. I can't seem to make sense of things.

It's the fever. It'll break. Do you have any idea how long you've been here?

She shook her head, asked: How long were you gone?

Overnight. One full day, the next morning. That was a week ago.

෴

She stayed awake much of that day, unsteady on her feet and with little strength, mostly sitting on the couch

with a blanket wrapped about her legs. Galen heated
water and in a washtub kneaded her clothes, some of
his, rinsed and wrung them out by hand, hung them to
dry on a line behind the cabin. When the day began to
wane he brought them inside and strung their hard-
frozen, flat scarecrow shapes across the room on a cord.
Jamie told him solemnly about her conversation with
Margaret's niece, of whom Galen had never heard. He
did not mention Jamie's feverish rantings or night-
marish wakings. When she began to doze, he roused her,
said: Into the loft with you.

   She protested, but he stopped her with a gesture, got
her to her feet. It's yours, he told her. You'll have privacy,
and it's warmer. He followed her up the stairs and she
stood in the loft's apex as he put a clean sheet on the mattress and folded two blankets at its foot, left her to lie
down, cover herself, sleep, went back downstairs and fed
the dog, then set about tidying the place, the sounds of his
movements becoming part of the aching course of her
blood. Once, he opened the door against the cabin's stuffy
heat and stood within it, at the fog's edge; and when he
turned around and faced the room he was struck as
though seeing it for the first time, through another's eyes,
a place not spartan but colorless, unrelieved.

   In prison Galen had learned how little a man needs.
A place to sleep, a place to relieve himself, a change of

clothes, food, a place to wash. *What prison really teaches you,* Galen's cellmate once told him, *is that there's nothing much you need. Nothing much material, anyway. Basics are basics.*

Galen looked about him, saw the threadbare couch, the tilting stovepipe, the worn table and scuffed chairs, the clothes drying on that cord, the bathroom door that had never hung evenly, the unpainted windowframes, sooty walls. He thought: This place is wretched. Then lost himself in the contemplation.

Sixteen

The hunter sat at his table, in the dim light of an oil lamp. He had no more use for electricity than he did for faucets; when he and his brother bought this place it had neither, and more than half a century later the sink's handpump was as good as new (its only problem being that it coughed up upon occasion baby mice senseless enough to have managed to drown) and the oil lamps still cast as much light as anyone who usually went to sleep just after nightfall and rose with the sun ever needed or wanted. The hunter leafed through a tattered journal that sufficed as his calendar—he had no need for storebought ones that only lasted a year—in which he kept track of the days by recording each in turn with his own laconic commentary, most entries not more than a line, two, and mostly unworthy of note except to some future meteorologist interested solely in the history of weather patterns over the north end of this watershed's reservoir.

The hunter long ago stopped noting dates, and though he sometimes wondered whether the *Monday* or *Thursday* or any other day he logged was truly that day, he also considered it hardly mattered either to him or to omniscient time itself. He examined with satisfaction his oval if childlike script, a hand unchanged since the last grade he ever completed, which was the sixth, flipped through the journal, paused to read here *Tuesday. Rained straight all day, shot a doe and her fawn* and there *Saturday. Very hot sun baking the land. Blackfly season,* and elsewhere *Monday. Heavy cloudcover spitting snow,* turned the dogeared pages and was assured that nothing of import had happened for a very long time. Though in the wooden chest pushed against one wall, other journals—of diverse sizes and with even more diverse bindings, some handstitched, all filled with the hunter's record of a life most cognizant of rain and snow and humidity, sunshine, nits and deerkills—contained cursory notations of personal tragedy as well as the weather, but the hunter had not perused these for many years and had no need to do so, for he needed no reminders; and being a solitary man since his younger brother's death many decades before, he was hardly tempted to summon a past only to despise it and to risk devastating his own restraint, which was such that on the day his brother died the hunter had merely chronicled *Sunday. My beloved Jordan dead today, early morning, God rest his soul. Raining horizontal sheets, windy, clouds low and flint colored.* The next day's entry read: *Monday. Sparse sunshine.*

The hunter did not consider the chest or the past now, thumbed through the tome before him and perused his notations of weather, mites and gnats, of pulling porcupine quills from the muzzle of one of his hounds, leafed through the meteorological minutiae of his everyday life, came to yesterday's entry, was satisfied. He wrote *Thursday.* below that, chewed on the pencil stub, looked about the room and wondered whether he must later undress in the dark, self-conscious as he was—as he'd always been since the accident that had scarred him from cheekbone to groin—of that purplish tissue raking down his face and chest and stomach. Not even his brother had ever seen him unshirted after it happened, nor had the hunter ever sought a wife; and he kept only one shard of mirror by the sink, enough to shave by, though he had little facial hair and preferred to remain unshaven rather than be reminded of that scar, which he believed to be a sure sign of God's displeasure, the mark of God's punishment, for as a young man he had been full of sin and weak before temptation. And

after being struck—struck down, he'd have said—the
hunter had hermitted himself away and then lived
through so many years that now almost no one was alive
who knew how he came by the scar, alone in the woods
and hard asleep with his back against the base of a mon-
strous oak, his gun beside him, singled out for his then-
unrepentant, repetitive trespasses—his love of
moonshine, his lust for loose women, those selfsame
women to whom he lost his only brother—by what the
hunter considered to be the vigilant Lord of divine and
merciless retribution. For how else to explain that deer
nuzzling him, the one he opened his eyes to witness
standing before him, waiting patiently for him to do
what God knew he would, catch that creature by a leg
with one hand and reach for his gun with the other so
that the deer did what God had planned for it to do,
sliced him open with one razorsharp hoof from cheekbone to gut and put such a mark on him that not even
Cain had borne. The hunter had cried out to the
Almighty then, the deer already off, away, and the
hunter's gun on the ground and him holding his
innards; and he'd survived, given up his evil ways, carried the sign of the Lord's displeasure upon him, known
the profundity that comes with divine punishment, that
of pure unadulterated humiliation. He'd survived—
purified and yet polluted—hermitted himself, and

hunted. Only deer, and with unyielding constancy.

But the hunter did not think of deer now; he thought of the act of undressing. He chomped on the pencil and spit out a minute splinter, set to writing. *Deep cold with damp, drizzle turning to wet snow,* he recorded. *Found a boy.*

⌒

The Lord works in mysterious ways, the hunter told himself when the boy, after stumbling into the blind of his own accord, began to follow him wordlessly, without forethought or afterthought, through the woods. The bloodsoaked, filthy material wrapped about the boy's hand held the hunter's attention, and he eyed that hand, the stained cloth, whenever he glanced back over his shoulder to assess the boy's progress as he staggered through the snow. They made slow going of it, did not reach the hunter's place until deep dusk. And there the hunter's two hounds bayed in the dogrun and leaped high along the fencing and pushed off it in awkward, leggy somersaults as the hunter opened the door to the shack, went in and set his rifle on its rack, lit two oil lamps, and returned outside to find the boy standing mesmerized before the crazed hounds.

They're good dogs, the hunter told him, come on in now. But the boy just stood where he was, so that the hunter had to herd him into the shack, stand him before the woodburning stove's thin warmth, from which the boy did not move even when the hunter worked at getting those few coals that still glowed to flame the new kindling, blowing on the embers until they caught, then putting in pieces of wood and setting the grate right.

The boy gazed at nothing, stood dumbly, did not take off his jacket, and so the hunter eventually peeled it from him, careful not to disturb that hand, hung the jacket on a peg and left to feed the hounds, returned to find the boy sitting on the floor in a corner and picking at the wrap, unraveling the soiled cloth that stuck one layer to the other much like old flypaper, the boy's earflap hat—too big for him by half, the hunter noted— low on his brow. The hunter came close when the boy dropped the mess beside him on the floor, saw that the peeled-back skin on his hand had already blackened around the edges, saw the thin discolored flesh and the boy's thumb bone, said: That needs cleaning. He set a kettle of water atop the stove and, before it quite steamed, took a piece of cord, pushed the boy's shirt-sleeve up, and tied the cord tight above the boy's elbow, the boy not looking at him or at anything, then poured the not-yet-boiling water onto a clean rag and did his best to wash out the wound, loosen and wipe away the dark clots within it.

You don't say much, the hunter remarked, the boy paying his ministrations no mind and his eyes remaining unfocused beneath that skewed hat, but maybe you will when that gets cauterized. And with that he took a small castiron frying pan and spooned some bacon grease into it, put it in place of the kettle on top of the stove, waited for the grease to melt and splatter. The boy did not seem to notice when the hunter approached, frying pan in hand. You might want to grit your teeth, the hunter said, stooping over him, then with a lightning-quick turn of the wrist poured the crackling grease onto the wound. At which the boy screamed and jumped up, yowling and grabbing his hand, tearing at the cord still tight around his arm, kicking and charging, the hunter moving faster than he had in years, getting out of the boy's enraged way.

Had to do that, the hunter said when the boy finally threw himself back down into the corner, cradling his hand and rocking, whimpering the while. The hunter left him alone, put more bacon fat into the pan. He fried some deer meat and made a flour gravy, set the mess onto two tin plates, put both on the table. The boy did not move from where he sat, still rocking, moaning now, the hunter eating slowly and watching him.

You better eat while it's hot, the hunter told him, and although the boy eventually tested the air like a dog, began to drool, he did not move out of the corner and so cringed when approached that the hunter put the plate on the floor by the boy's feet, dared come no closer. But by the time the hunter opened his journal, the boy had reached with his good hand toward the plate, tentatively touching the meat with his fingers to check its heat before gobbling it down.

Take your hat off, for it seems that the Good Lord intends for you to stay, the hunter said after he entered his notation for the day. The boy paid him no mind, and the hunter blew out the oil lamp's flame, considered the hand of God, undressed in the dark, and let the boy be.

Seventeen

Winter's rains fell. Galen slept on the couch, kept the fire burning, watched Jamie, still pallid from fever and with dark circles under her eyes, come and go from the loft. Midmorning on the second day of downpour the dog rose from before the woodburning stove, woofed ferociously. Galen opened the door and peered out into the deluge, palmed the dog's muzzle and tapped its nose, told it to stay, be quiet, closed it within the cabin and walked the porch's length. Harlan came toward him, hatted and head down and watching his footing as he sloshed through the midcalf-deep slush of the unplowed and untended drive, rifle in hand. When he got close enough he looked up at Galen, cursed, said: I should've known.

Known what?

That you were here.

He stepped up onto the porch as Galen blocked the

door. Damn this weather, Harlan told him, sweeping the
stained, widebrimmed leather hat from his head and
shaking it and putting it back on, then gesturing with
the gun. It's all still here, ain't it, Harlan remarked,
unquestioning. It took me a while to figure it out, did
some asking around. Damn, but this brings back memories now, don't it?

Galen folded his arms.

The good ol' days, buddy.

Something tells me you didn't come to reminisce,
Harlan.

The dog pawed at the door from inside, growled.
Harlan smirked, shook his head. You're smarter than
that, you sonovabitch. You've already figured why I'm
here, so just go on in there and trot him out.

Who?

Harlan barked a humorless half-laugh. That's good,
he admitted. Your act's good.

It's no act.

Don't waste my time, Galen. I came for the boy.

There's no boy here.

Oh yeah? Well, the dog's in there.

A dog is in there. So what?

Her dog, I'm betting. Which means she's in there.
Which means the boy's in there. Or, Harlan gestured
with the rifle again and looked around, somewhere here.

You're wrong.

And you're lying. 'Cause I saw the tracks above Margaret's place, three sets of them. Yours and hers, the dog's, the boy's.

That's four.

I ain't here to do arithmetic. Just open the door.

Galen stood his ground, watched Harlan's expression darken as his knuckles about the rifle tightened, whitened. The girl and dog came on their own, Galen said, by themselves.

You can either open the door or get yourself killed. Your choice.

Galen turned and opened the door a crack, spoke to the dog, kneed his way in to keep the creature in check, then collared and dragged it toward the counter. Harlan pushed into the cabin, said: You better hold that mutt good.

Leave the gun outside, Galen said tensely. The dog twisted, squirmed, trying to wriggle free of his grip. Jamie, confused by the commotion, looked down from the edge of the loft, went paler than Galen ever thought possible as the blood drained from her face at the sight of Harlan.

The gun, Galen repeated. Harlan ignored him, stalked across the room, looked into the small bathroom, flung opened the closet door, climbed the stairs to

the loft, saw she was alone. Get down, he said. You hold
that dog, he yelled at Galen as she climbed down
unsteadily, and you, he told Jamie, go stand by the
couch. She did what he said, trembling not from fever or
cold but from terror's stranglehold, Harlan raising the
rifle waist-high and training it on Galen and the dog,
that gun throttling her innocence—for that innocence
that impels youth's resolve to experience and survive
each moment and every emotion magnified tenfold or a
hundredfold or a thousandfold was now wholly gar-
roted, dead within her, displaced by the frightening,
unambiguous knowledge of pure vulnerability.

They're dead if I don't get some answers, Harlan
snapped at her. Where's the boy?

Harlan, Galen said, she's going to come over here
and hold the dog, and then you and I are going out.
We'll walk over every inch of ground. You can check the
stables and sheds, look everywhere. And when you find
nothing we'll go back the way they came, and if there are
any tracks left in this slush we'll follow them, and you'll
see hers and the dog's and maybe mine but no one else's.
Because I snowshoed in days before she did, and when
she got here the only thing with her was the dog.

You better say something right quick, Harlan told
her, the rifle still held waist-high, trained.

She hasn't seen the boy, Galen insisted. I haven't

seen the boy. And he's not here.

Say something, bitch.

Jamie, come here, Galen said, come hold the dog. Galen nodded at her soberly, almost spoke again before she moved, her legs unsteady, before she covered the distance between them without even knowing it, collapsed onto her knees and put her arms around the dog, held it tightly.

I'm getting my jacket, Galen told Harlan, and then Harlan stepped back, watched Galen sling his jacket over a shoulder, open the door. You coming or not? Galen asked.

Jamie let go of the dog after they left and, still quaking, got to her feet, shakily crossed over to the grimed windows and watched the two men go back and forth, from one rundown stable and shed to another. They eventually headed for the carousel, vanished beyond it, the rain bucketing down. The dog paced before the threshold, distressed, whining. Jamie waited a long time—the time not quelling her terror but after a while allowing her to suffer only sporadic shudders—by the window before exhaustion prodded her to move to the couch, where she remained, barely noticing the dog eventually settle at her feet and so dazed that she hardly knew that she sat there straining to hear a sound, any sound, in dread of hearing a shot.

Galen finally came back, solitary, dripping, bolting the door behind him, stripping off his jacket and pulling off his sodden boots before going over to her, crouching, placing a hand on her forehead.

Where is he? she asked.

Gone, Galen answered. He looked so thoughtfully at her and in such a way that for a fleeting second she was reminded of Margaret's photograph of him as a boy, his arm crooked effortlessly about a ewe's neck, the seriousness within his dark, inscrutable eyes. And then Galen was on his feet, at the counter. He boiled water, made tea, rolled a cigarette.

He won't be back, he told her.

How do you know?

Because there's no sign of the boy. He gave up sloshing around out there before I did. There's no reason for him to return.

I'm afraid of him.

Don't be, Galen said, then thought of the shot that had reverberated endlessly, of the way Bobby's girl had crumpled and how he had tried to stem the blood flowing from her chest, the way her fingers had twitched and stilled and how sightlessness had veiled her eyes. Galen passed a hand over his face, remembered the numbing shock that had dulled him, remembered the way he had lain beside her as though his life too were ebbing.

The boy's out there, Jamie said.

Galen shook his head. There's no one out there.

He's out there, Galen. He tried to put the dog into some kind of harness. I know it was him, it had to be him. The dog got away and came back, and I got the harness off and then we left Margaret's. But the boy followed me, the dog. At least as far as that quarry along the way.

You dreamed that.

It wasn't a dream.

Galen lit the cigarette, leaned back against the counter, met her eyes. Look, he finally said, if the boy's out there, he's cold and wet and miserable. And far from here. Far from anywhere Harlan's looking.

But what if

Don't ask, Galen stopped her. He did not want to say what did not need saying. The raindrops slanted hard against the windows, like an assault of tears.

⤸

Jamie tossed and turned under the roof-tapping rain and slept intermittently, dreaming of water flowing over minksoft grasses bent under rivulets, of fish swaying in undulating currents, of waterfalls rainbowing. At times her fever surged, and she'd come to her senses drenched, listen to the overhead downpour hush and drum, then drift on the sound and muse on how just two generations past it was rain that determined the reservoir's meteoric rise, rain that melted away winter year in and year out to swell with winter's vestiges those creeks from which raging waters poured forth into the river, the river emptying into the valley and its waters backflowing after coming up against the dam upon which the causeway lay, flooding backward and slowly submerging the last traces of the valley settlement that now was as irretrievable as the residues of flesh from the graves of those who watched the rising waters. Occasionally, when her fever lessened, Jamie slept an otherworldly twilight sleep, aware of the rain's ceaseless and varied patterns that made her bones echo to the rhythms on the roof that were at times no more than a whispered patter and at other times a relentless throb, and she sometimes imagined herself to be an animal in its lair, patient and impatient for the rain to stop, for the shape of things to come to be revealed.

And then her fever broke, with her awake at dawn before realizing that she had woken, for the last wisps of dream—of her grandmother in wet, clinging clothes sitting on a granite outcrop next to her mother, who from a picnic basket pulled colorful ribbons the length of which could not plumb the lake's depths—were slow to dissipate. She looked over the loft's edge, saw with a

touch of surprise the empty couch, watched the wan
light rub up against the gray window for an unsustain-
able moment, one which time and nature collaborated
to arrest before allowing the day to move on, become.
She was already down from the loft when Galen came
through the door with an armful of wood, said to him,
Leave it open, the air feels good.

She stood in the doorway, tested the porch's damp,
cool planking with a bare foot, surveyed a world much
changed: the sodden snow no longer deep, the swollen
creek seeping onto its banks and pooling a shallow pond
that reached almost to the merry-go-round, the glis-
tening leantos and sheds and tumbledown rails and
fences, and the long, rising knoll of what had once been
an open meadow but was now full of wetly glinting
brush, the dripping forest beyond. She breathed in
deeply and watched the dog splash toward her, breathed
in deeply and studied the soft overcast sky.

I'm starving, she murmured. Galen made breakfast,
and she devoured what he set before her, sitting in the
clothes she'd slept in for what seemed ages, her hair tou-
sled, tangled. Galen drew up one knee, rested an elbow on
it, watched her wordlessly, and she was struck by the fact
that he was a man who was easy with silence, easy too
with listening. He had been mostly silent at Margaret's,
had always listened, Margaret doing the talking while he

repaired a patch of pumphouse siding or turned over
the earth in the garden or stripped windows and doors;
mostly silent even when he and Margaret would walk
together, even when they sat on the porch, Galen evi-
dencing his undivided attention by tilting his head just
so, looking now and then at Margaret in just such a way,
easy and comfortable but mindful nonetheless; mostly
silent not because he was shy—he wasn't—but because
he weighed on the most sensitive of scales those words
he might speak against that hush he might violate and
almost always tipped that scale in favor of silence.

Jamie finished eating, wiped her fingers, pushed a
strand of hair behind her ear in a self-mocking way,
raised her coffee mug to Galen, said: I must be a sight.

Indeed, he returned. Thinking he'd never in his life
seen anyone, anything, so lovely.

↜

Galen was astonished, disconcerted too, by how
effortlessly they slipped into the tranquil embrace of
domesticity: for here they were, the dog before the
woodburning stove, the days wearing on uninterrupted
in a wintry season, the spoken and unspoken between
them disturbing nothing. Not that he wasn't intensely
aware of everything she did or of the shape of her shoulders and the hollow just above her clavicle, the way she

pulled her hair back from her face with those fine hands,
the way she moved, glided, about, how she left transfor-
mation in her wake—atop the table now a chipped
porcelain vase of juniper cuttings, jars arranged on the
counter like a still life, trunks opened and searched
through and a filmy stretch of muslin found, hung from
the loft, a baby's quilt patterned in vibrant reds, yellows,
cornflower blue tacked onto a downstairs wall, Jamie
sometimes standing before it as though reading a map,
as though its patchwork maze illustrated those future
passageways that would one day claim her. As she did
now, Galen across the room and leaning against the
counter, watching her back.

You never said, he ventured, where you were from.

She did not turn around. To name it would mean
nothing, would not describe those select iconic moments
somehow precedent within the void of time's passing,
those memories within her that gave the town, gave her
too, meaning: a lone girl with pigtails wearing a torn
dress skipping along a sidewalk beside the garbage-
strewn, algae-blooming canal; the glinting ice chips in
the runners of the iceman's cart; her mother's hand
holding hers while they crossed a street and her mother
laughing because Jamie had asked her to reach up high,
touch a cloud; the bear standing on the curb waiting
patiently for Jamie and her mother to recross the street,

retrieve the imaginary creature; that first kiss in a far schoolyard corner and the freckles on the boy's nose; the thin peanut-butter sandwiches in her lunchbox; the heifer that escaped the slaughterhouse and loped past the window at exactly the moment Jamie looked up from drawing a map of Chile; home economics classes for two years every school Friday, of which Jamie remembers only the smell and taste of hot dogs sliced and stuffed with cheese, wrapped in bacon; the wooden bleachers around the football field, gangly boys revving the engines of their rebuilt jalopies, the girls who wanted to be beauty queens; the bursting sweetness of fried clam bellies; the sight of her mother's friends with their bleached teased hair and Cleopatra-like mascara and each of them misshapen, too thin or too squat, at her gravesite. That was where Jamie considered she was from: a place of discordant memories. And she thought of how the last of the mills closed during her childhood, how the Main Street stores one after the other were boarded except for the secondhand shops, the junkshops; how the highway that passed the town sprang malls and shopping centers and left the town's center to die. How people tried to get by and mostly did, like her mother had, but just barely.

Jamie shrugged, responded, Just a town, probably like most others. A nowhere place.

Where? Galen asked.

In another state.

He took his time, asked: Do you think of going back?

She turned to face him, shook her head. He shifted slightly, told her offhandedly: When I was first away from here, in the service, I thought I'd never come back. Thought I'd settle somewhere else, start over somewhere else.

And?

My father was here. This place was here. In the end, I couldn't stop thinking about it.

You had someone, something to come back to, she remarked. That makes all the difference.

And you don't?

Jamie paused. Not dropping her eyes, not looking elsewhere, but that pause almost made Galen hold his breath. And then she said, My mother's dead.

I know, he reminded her. What about your father?

She paused again, shrugged again. Just gone, I guess. I don't even know how we ended up where we did, in that town. I don't know where he came from, how they met. All I know is what my mother told me.

Which was?

That one day he left, not saying he wouldn't be back. My mother never said, but I know that she thought by staying put he'd be able to find us again if he ever decided, needed, wanted to. So she—we—stayed put. And then she got sick. I quit school, tried to make ends meet. And then she died.

And you left.

If I'd stayed, they would have taken the dog. I would have gone to a foster home. So I headed for Dyers Corner.

Of all places.

It was the only other place I'd ever been. Just a stop along the way.

Well, Galen said after a moment, with studied nonchalance, it's a big world.

Yeah, she remarked with a shrug, walking over to the door. She let the dog out, saw the icicles rimming the porch roof, the tinseled branches of the far pines, the creek that, having overflowed its banks, silvered a frozen expanse before the carousel. Galen, she said, let's go out, and without waiting for him pulled on her boots, jacket. He followed, watching her test the ice beneath the skim of the surface and half walk, half mock-skate toward the merry-go-round. When she reached the carousel, she stepped up and stood among the carved horses halted in somnambulant stampede. The dog frolicked, raced back and forth between the carousel and Galen, leaped onto the merry-go-round as Galen straddled the back of a horse and licked at the mount's flared nostrils.

A big world, Jamie echoed, repeated.

So I hear, Galen said. Sometimes made up of small places. Mostly, maybe. Though probably none as small as this.

And this place is—she spread her arms, turned a slow circle—beautiful.

It's the light, Jamie. The winter softens everything derelict.

And in the summer, when there's a moon?

Then maybe it's beautiful, Galen admitted. Definitely more forlorn.

She walked around, touching a carved mane here, a bunched hindquarter there, came back to where Galen perched. She fingered his mount's ears, studied its widely round peeling eyes.

Was there music when it worked? Lights?

Galen nodded. And rings to catch.

Rings?

Over there, on that pole. The outside riders always grabbed for them, tried to slip them off a hook.

What for?

Because they were wishing rings.

So if you got one, you got a wish?

Galen nodded.

And would it come true?

Almost never.

She glided over to the pole, saw where the hook had once been embedded. Too bad there aren't any rings left.

Just put your hands on the pole and close your eyes, Galen told her. Wish hard for something. Anything at all. But for one thing.

Jamie put her hands on the pole and tilted her head back, closed her eyes, then took her hands away, looked at Galen expectantly.

Want to know what I wished?

I don't think you're supposed to tell.

Then guess.

Peace on earth. Fresh vegetables on your plate.

Be serious.

I am serious.

I wished—Galen held up his hands to stop her—that I could be somebody.

You are somebody.

She shook her head. I'm not anybody at the moment. Not even a housekeeper.

Well, Galen told her, then maybe it's time you became an equestrian.

His remark so startled her that she laughed, a deep and throaty sound, as she moved away from the pole. She walked around the merry-go-round, touching the horses' heads with one finger as though with a wand, and Galen, wondering at the wonder of it, realized he'd

never heard her laugh before, never seen her take a
moment so lightly; and then she was back at his side,
amused and bemused and enchanting, too close. He
slipped off the horse, holding himself from her at arm's
length, leaned against another. Jamie threw a leg over his
horse's back, sat, raised her knees as though she were a
jockey, leaned forward, tilted her head and looked at
him, the laughter in her eyes yet.

Maybe I'll do just that, she said. In Margaret's honor.

Stay, Galen almost said, did not say. The dog left
them, bounded a few strides into the snow, stopped and
leaned into its forward stance. They saw the hunter then,
a piece of canvas shawled over his jacket and with a
piece of deer hind slung, hooked, over his shoulder. Had
he hooded the canvas over his head as well, the hunter
would have looked like some harbinger of death from
another age—a mendicant grave digger, dishonorable
grave robber—rather than what he appeared to be, an
ancient and lone pioneer without buckskin or fringe.
The hunter did not see them until Galen called out, and
then he raised one acknowledging hand curtly and continued his stubborn trajectory toward the cabin.

They met him on the porch, the hunter handing
Galen the meat, hook and all, taking the canvas from his
shoulders, crooking his head at an ungainly angle and
hunching to hide as much of the scar as possible. He

touched a finger to his cap, said: Good to see you and that dog got here.

Thanks to you, Jamie replied, Galen looking in surprise at both.

Thought you could use that, the hunter remarked to Galen.

It's much appreciated, Galen responded. Come in for a cup of coffee.

No need, the hunter told him, but he followed them in and took a chair. I won't be staying, so don't go to any bother, he protested as Jamie busied herself with the percolator. Actually, I was hoping you might have something on hand I could use on one of my hounds that got cut on some barbed wire somewhere. The wound is festering. I did have a jar with a skull and crossbones on it somewhere, but I have to admit I can't figure where it went to.

All I can think of giving you, Galen told him, is what whiskey I've got. It'll do, maybe, as an antiseptic.

That would be better than nothing, the hunter reflected. Galen went to a cupboard, brought out a bottle of whiskey, placed it on the table. And then they spoke of how best to clean and soak and dress the wound, whether to trim away the dead flesh and how deeply to cut, and when the coffee was ready Jamie brought two cups to the table and returned to the counter, sipped hers with her back to them. The hunter blew on his and kept his face to one side. Galen asked the condition of the reservoir's ice.

Depends on where you're standing, as always, the hunter replied. I've never known that lake to freeze over completely, and there's plenty of open water. You've got to know what you're doing out there. You planning on ice-fishing?

It occurred to me, Galen answered.

Well, you be careful if you do, the hunter warned before downing his coffee in several gulps and abruptly getting to his feet. Thank you for this. I should be heading back to tend to that dog now.

Jamie, still standing at the counter, asked over her shoulder, By the way, did you ever see that boy?

Boy? the hunter echoed.

The one I told you about. Who was at the quarry.

No ma'am, the hunter replied, pocketing the bottle of whiskey, then said to Galen: I'm grateful for this.

It's nothing. Considering the meat, not even a fair trade.

That hound means a good deal to me, the hunter assured him. Don't bother getting up.

No bother, Galen remarked, let me walk you out. And they left, went past the sheds and stables, Galen matching the hunter's pace. There's no need for you to be accompanying me, the hunter noted, unless you have something on your mind.

As a matter of fact, I have. You see, I didn't realize you and the girl had crossed paths. She never told me.

Well, it probably wasn't worthy of mention. Though it's good that she stumbled onto the blind. The snow was coming down heavy, and she wasn't quite sure of the way.

And she told you she'd seen a boy?

She said something to that effect.

Galen stopped, and the hunter paused. That boy's from the junkyard at The Bend, Galen told him. He's been missing for a while.

It's a bad season to go missing in.

It is. I'd appreciate you letting me know if you come across him.

Be glad to, the hunter replied, shaking Galen's out-stretched hand in farewell, going on alone. Wondering the while it took him to reach his shack what punishment would be wrought upon him for telling such lies.

∽

Galen made Jamie recount how she and the dog had come across the hunter's blind, said nothing for a long while, decided.

What are you thinking? she asked.

That I'd better have a look, he told her. The rain has

probably washed everything away, but if not, I might be able to tell what direction the boy took.

And if you can?

Then it'll be a long day. A longer one if I come across him.

I'll come with you.

No. You stay here, keep resting, keep the stove going. I'll take the dog, if you want.

I'm rested.

You're not well enough to go as far as The Bend on foot. Which is where I'll end up if I find him.

You'd bring him back there?

I'd bring him just about anywhere I had to, just so we can put all this behind us.

We, Jamie repeated, as though she had never heard the word before. Us, she repeated, as though the word were a bitter almond in her mouth.

You, Galen amended, the dog, me. Plural: we, us.

⌐

The quarry had been pelted hard, and Galen saw no sign of the boy, though beyond the blind he thought he found the hunter's curiously trampled tracks, which he followed for a while until they were simply lost. And then Galen headed back in the afternoon's gloom, unable to shake himself free of that cautionary tone with which she'd repeated *We. Us.* and coming up hard against knowing that he should not—not ever—assume or even imagine a *we* or *us*, conjure any hope from whatever happenstance or abject need had brought her to him. He tried to steel himself against the inevitable, told himself that Jamie would not and could not stay, admonished himself that she could not, should not choose to live her life with a man exactly twice her age whose emotions and experiences were in no way, in no way reflected, her own. Galen walked rapidly, hands thrust into his pockets and the dog—*her* dog, he reminded himself—before him, Galen wanting to stop time, disallow the future, so that neither he nor Jamie would have to confront or define— which meant exploding—that *we, us.* And he rebelled with every step against the thought of losing her, the thought of her leaving.

He pondered whether he should tell her what he had learned in prison, that the world was divided into loners and those who were lonely, and that he knew himself to be both; pondered too how to explain to her that he detested both, that within prison and then outside of it he had simply learned to live with the grating grind of solitude, with a wasted emptiness spawned of solitude, but that he had never reconciled himself to either. And now more than ever did not want to.

What goes around comes around, Galen's cellmate

always said, *it's all a grand design.* And finding in Galen
a nonbeliever, his cellmate constantly taunted him,
spoke of lifetimes past and unrecognizable in their
present reenactments, their immediate reincarnations.
*We've met before, we've all met before, everyone in your
life you've met before, you're just living out the tally sheet
of what you owe and what's owed to you, that's all,* he
always said, *we're just here to even out the score.* Days and
evenings and weeks and months, years, went by, and
Galen listened to him, answered him with silence,
named the snowfalls. During the winters Galen
dreamed of forests and the mountain range's endless
expanse, and in all seasons found it futile to grapple
with the unknowable, with all that could not be determined. Look, Galen once told his cellmate early on and
in pure exasperation, shut up. All I want to do is forget.

What are you in for? his cellmate asked then.

An accident, Galen answered.

There's no such thing, he was told.

The dog frisked before Galen, at times nosed its way
along, at times trotted with its head and tail up, the frost
on its coat silvery. When Galen reached the knoll, the
dog broke into a lope and Galen took a deep breath, two,
tried to gather his wits, judge how to say what he
wanted, needed, to tell her, passed by the poled horses
standing at attention above the merry-go-round's

warped floor, passed through his past. Decided that he
could not, would not, say anything.

And so he opened the door wordlessly and stepped
inside and saw the dog go to her, her back to him and
rinsing dishes, saw that she did not take a towel and dry
her hands, reach down to pet the dog, greet it. Jamie did
not turn around, and her posture seemed strangely
rigid. And then she said in a voice so low that Galen
thought he had not heard her at all: Harlan was here.

Galen stared at her back, asked after a moment:
What did he want?

The boy, she answered, her voice still low, even,
controlled. You weren't here, the dog wasn't here. That
convinced him that you were with the boy, that we're
hiding him.

He's crazy.

He said he'd be back. And that the boy better be here
when he returns, or else.

Or else what?

He said you'd ask that, she remarked. And turned to
him then, her lip split, one blackened eye already
swollen, her cheek cut, bruised.

Eighteen

The boy did not consider himself to be found or lost, saved or unsaved, nor did he consider more than his immediate surroundings, the murkiness within the shack and the excruciatingly painful throb to his hand that now ate into his wrist and forearm, into his armpit. He listened without comprehending to the hunter's words, as words held no meaning for and were undistinguished by the boy except as cadenced noise; but the hunter's movements were something that kept the boy wary. He cowered whenever the hunter cooked, bared his teeth when the hunter came too close to him, drew his knees up sharply and kept them before his chest and protected his hand then, pulled down the hat that already sat low and askew on his brow. The hunter had to throw him pieces of bread, or leave a plate of whatever he cooked on the floor somewhere near the boy.

The boy did not consider the world beyond the shack's interior except when the hunter went outside and left the door open, for then the boy would get to his feet and, swaying, go to the threshold, sniff the air, be held there by the sound of the noisy hounds and the sight of them within their pen, the dogs bounding at the hunter and tearing at the pieces of raw meat he dropped onto the ground. The hunter just stood there as the snarling dogs gulped their feed until they finished and began to leap about again, again howling crazily, and he always had to knee and kick at them as he backed his way out of the pen. The boy would back up then too, as though he and the hunter were connected by some invisible wire, ignore the hunter's beckoning wave, his call, watch as he went to the smokehouse where deer shanks and ribs and shoulders hung from the rafters. And then the boy would lose interest in the hounds—his hand and wrist, forearm and armpit burning—and move back into the shack and for no reason the hunter could imagine pull out drawers, search through cupboards, empty them of their curious contents. One day the boy broke a vial underfoot and noticed small, sparkling silver balls quivering, rolling around. He squatted, fascinated by the mercury, and with his good hand pushed the drops together, squished them apart with a finger, rolled them back together again; and before the hunter returned from the smokehouse, the boy had scooped what mercury he could into his useless hand, returned to his corner. When the hunter walked in, he saw the crushed vial, what was left on the floor, looked at the boy, shook his head, almost took the Lord's name in vain, then swept the mercury out of the shack with a rough handbroom, the drops cascading madly. Afterward, the hunter tried to edge toward the boy, stopped when the boy growled, watched him stare at his wounded hand and the mercury he held in it.

That there's for anyone who's gotten sick from a woman, the hunter remarked, and what would you know of that.

The boy opened, closed his mouth, pressed the mercury into the wound with the fingers of his good hand. Whether the coldness of the viscous liquid or the way it shined pleased him, the hunter could not tell. When that gets into your blood you'll froth at the mouth like a rabid dog, he warned. And then shook his head at the boy's incomprehension.

ᔑ

Temperature below freezing, punked snowpack icy, the hunter recorded. He brought the pencil to his mouth, bit into it, touched the scar on his cheek with one finger, looked up from the table. The boy sat drooling in the corner with a vacant expression and graying pallor, his head against the wall and his oozing hand palm up on his knees. Bubbles lathered the corners of his mouth.

Was a time, the hunter said, motioning toward the boy's hand, when Doc Buzzard made his rounds to minister to such things. He'd come rowing across the reservoir dressed like a preacher, blacksuited and with a white collar. He had the biggest Adam's apple and longest neck I've ever seen, and birdlike eyes, and he'd listen to your heart and hammer at your joints and bleed you with leeches for some things and cup you for others, cut buckshot out from wherever you needed it cut out, deliver babies, pull teeth, sell elixirs and balms and ointments, take payment when he could get it, in currency or in kind. We always paid him in liquor, and he'd put that jug down beside his black satchel on the floor of that rowboat and off he'd go, looking more like a vulture than a man, long arms pumping like wings as he rowed away. I never knew him by any other name, and if he ever had one he must have disowned it, for Doc Buzzard suited him fine.

The boy rolled his head from side to side. You could stand to see the likes of him now, the hunter went on. That wrist's streaking badly. Doc Buzzard could have done something for you, I'm sure. I would have died if it hadn't been for him. My insides were outside.

The hunter averted his face then, aware that he had been looking at the boy squarely. He reached for the oil lamp and lowered the flame, closed the journal before him, set the pencil down. Doc said he'd never seen any such thing in his life, said he never even heard of a deer doing that to a man, swore he'd never put so many stitches in a single body in all his years. He worked on me a long time, seared me like I did you, melted down pigfat on this same stove and mentioned that any grease would do, said that in the old days pioneers would use the fat from dead Indians if they had to. That struck me as hard, I must say. Flaying a man even if he's dead is a terrible thing. Almost as terrible as the pain when Doc poured that grease on, set to work sewing me up. Stitching is probably what you need, but I'm sorry to say I can't do that for you.

The boy remained a study in vacuity, worked his mouth, gurgled a froth that resembled thinly beaten eggwhites. That's the mercury, the hunter remarked. Like I told you, that isn't for what ails you, it's for treating the sickness you get from women. My brother suffered from that, and Doc Buzzard treated him. He always said like cured like, that poison cured poison.

The boy fixed the hat on his head with his good hand, closed his eyes. Whatever you tussled with, the hunter remarked, that mercury won't do you any good.

Nineteen

Jamie watched Galen pack a skinning knife and tobacco and matches and snares, a small aluminum pot, food and socks and sweaters. Next to his backpack he placed a small ax, rope—for he had decided that the boy who was once tied might have to be tied again, might not come with them on his own—moleskin, the two sleeping bags he unrolled and shook out and rerolled. He set about replacing a worn strap on one of the snow-shoes. We don't need these now, but we will, he told her when he finished, then packed her knapsack with what he wanted her to carry.

You should get some sleep, he said later, but she could not sleep for the dread, for her fear that Harlan might appear in the night, and long before dawn she climbed down from the loft and found Galen awake too, sitting on the couch. She sat beside him without saying a word and without throwing a light switch, for she did not want him to see her face again: his fury was already barely containable. She did not ask him how long he thought they might be gone—as long, she assumed, as needed to find the boy or determine that he could not be found.

Jamie did not ask what would happen if they did not find him, and Galen did not say. She thought she already knew: she would walk away from this place, away from the brush she had had with Galen's life, leave penniless and with the dog and a knapsack holding the few things belonging to her. She did not know that Galen sensed this—he did—and that he inwardly both raged and despaired, his desperation sparked by his certainty that Jamie would also leave if they found the boy, his rage fueled by his hatred for Harlan. Who had once again stepped in to unravel—undo—Galen's life. Galen purely hating too what he could not get out of his mind, his cellmate saying, *We just keep going in circles that just get tighter and tighter. Our lives senselessly repeating themselves within themselves over and over.*

Just before dawn and without speaking, Galen got up and turned on the lights, checked her knapsack, his backpack, strapped onto them their sleeping bags. As the sky began to glimmer he damped the coals in the woodburning stove and rolled a cigarette, opened the door, stood leaning against it, smoked. She went and stood beside him, grave, intent. Sorry, she said, this is all my doing. And he studied her impassively, waited for her to say: And when it's over, we'll just get on with our lives, you with yours, me with mine. But she said nothing more, and he took in her welted face, her split lip, bruised and cut cheek, blackened eye, wanted nothing else than for her to say that she would not walk away from him no matter what, longed for the impossible. And then he let go. He felt the break and the heartbreak and he let go, accepted the fact that she would vanish, was meant to vanish. He dropped the cigarette onto the porch, crushed it underfoot, said: You did what you thought was right. Said: It's time to wrap your ankles.

They closed the door behind them and the dog lifted its head and watched as she sat and Galen knelt before her, wound the moleskin carefully about her ankles so they would not chafe, his hands pausing in midair just as he finished because Jamie—moved by this unexpected, gentle intimacy—leaned toward him, cupped her hand under his chin thinking *I will let this much happen, because it should happen, was bound to happen, must happen now before it is too late for it to happen at all,* and brought her bruised mouth to his, kissed him. The kiss tentative, tender, unbearable. And he said: Oh god Jamie don't.

He pulled away from her and they put on their
boots and jackets. He helped her with the knapsack,
checked its weight and the lay of the shoulderstraps,
packed the ax into its sidepocket, hooked one pair of
snowshoes onto the back of the knapsack, sent her outside. He got his backpack on with the other pair of
snowshoes, glanced outside, saw that she stood facing
away, closed his eyes and passed a hand over his mouth
in an effort to dispel the intimation of her lips on his,
took a deep breath, walked out. He locked the door
behind him, passed her by where she stood with her
hands in her pockets, Jamie not looking at him. The dog
wagged its tail, followed him. Galen set a steady pace.
Jamie fell in behind and beyond the merry-go-round
paused, the melancholy flooding through her—as it did
the moment Galen so reacted to her kiss—deepening at
the sight of those magnificent steeds beaten down by the
brunt of time.

⌐

It was Galen's intention to sweep the mountainsides
above the reservoir, traversing back and forth as they
wound their way higher and higher, as much in the hope
of finding a sign of the boy as in the hope that the boy
would espy the dog, show himself. Galen did not lead

the way to the blind or the quarry, but above both began to contour along a deer trail and tracked it easily through dense firs whose boughs rebounded and swayed when he knocked the snow from them with his passing. Jamie kept to his pace, watched his gracefulness and his watchfulness, tried to see what it was he saw, paused where he paused and surveyed what he surveyed and then pushed on, one behind the other and both as silent as stalkers. The crusted snowpack proved treacherous at times, and when it did she kept her head down, concentrated on her footing, leaned forward away from the weight of her knapsack, balanced herself; and when the rough going lessened she marveled at the unbroken expanse of wilderness cascading away from them in all directions and seemingly forever. Galen did not look back at her until they began to make their way around a ridge's ledges whose nooks and crannies sprouted moss of an impossibly emerald hue beneath a thin, icy veneer, and then he paused, checked her progress, asked whether the weight on her back were shifting—it was— and readjusted the knapsack's straps without meeting her eye, then led on. They climbed toward the treeline above which the cloudcover curled an ashen lip over the mountains before descending away from both to push on along something that seemed to be a trail but upon which nothing had walked for several snows. Eventually they came to a clearing from where they could see the forest and mountainsides slope downward for an inestimable distance and, below, the reservoir, its alabaster surface darkly veined with coalblack streaks of open water. The dog dug at the snow, chewed pieces it managed to dislodge, and Galen stomped about and kicked free thin shards of snowcrust that they held in their hands and sucked.

Where are we?

Pretty far above the quarry, Galen answered, not looking at her. Quite a way beyond it.

Where are we going?

Back and forth. Covering the distance between The Bend—he pointed in one direction—and my place— pointed in another—and climbing higher with each pass.

Good, she remarked, her response so surprising to him that he turned his head, saw that she meant it, saw too the color in her cheeks and a stunning clarity to her eyes; and she smiled a small smile, looked at her feet, seemed unmindful of her battered face, unmindful even of the cold. Good, she said again, glanced meaningfully at him, for she was content with the going, untroubled as a young animal reveling in unconscious delight at its own body, at the sheer joy of movement. And Galen realized that Jamie was relieved—no, happy—to be far

from the cabin, at peace with—no, delighted by—the
wilderness, for here she thought she was beyond rules,
even beyond relying on the kindness of strangers (Margaret's favorite line from a play she'd once seen, which
she always quoted to Galen), a dependence Jamie would
have to give in to once she hit the road again. But here,
now, Jamie thought she was free, as she understood
nothing of the mountain range's hostility, none of
nature's deceits and dangers. *That* was what the kiss was
about, Galen told himself, realized insanely: she knew
she was about to walk away from who she was and who
she might become, knew she could ignore for at least a
splice of time the fact that tomorrow or the day after or
three days from now she'd be confronted once again
with the immediate it humdrum reality of moving on.
And Galen realized too, insanely still, that he forgave her
that smile, her joy—if that was what it was—begrudged
her nothing except that kiss and all that it had
unleashed, unsettled, within him.

Ready? he asked, and she nodded. They went on and
the day wore on, the sky thickening with cloudcover, the
cold pressing. They zigzagged long lengths and wound
their way upward through the mountains, taking breaks
but not for long, seeing no sign of the boy. Jamie tried to
guess the way, tried to understand what Galen conjured
from the warp and weave of the land as he read the

wilderness for passage, ascertained difficulties better avoided than encountered, went on in the same unhurried, determined pace. Once, she saw their footprints far below them, heading in the opposite direction, and was awed: for she had no sense that they had turned anywhere, gone anywhere but up. And once, when she found herself lagging, tiring, she asked if this were the only way to wherever it was they were going.

No, Galen told her, it's the longer way.

And she looked about her, shook her head, said: This is crazy.

What is? That we're sweeping?

No. That you can figure this out, know where to go.

We're on trails. They're mostly everywhere; it's just a matter of recognizing them. After all, people once moved throughout these mountains, hunted them, crossed them. They even—once upon a time—lived here. Or at least some did.

And now?

Now there's just whatever they left behind. Paths. A shelter here and there, sometimes a shack. Leantos.

And no one.

Not that I've seen yet, he said dryly, but we've a way to go. And then he continued on, as before, and toward the end of the day they passed stands of pine and juniper before breaking out onto an expanse of frozen

beaver ponds, around which bark-stripped treetrunks
and gnawed stumps jutted above the ice. Galen
motioned for her to follow, then pushed on, Jamie
walking where he walked as they moved quickly over the
level surfaces of interlocking marshes, one higher than
the next, the dead trees and jagged stumps taking on
phantom shapes in the dying light. She heard water flow
beneath the dams, saw Galen reach a mounded beaver
lair and toe its base, watched the dog make its way over
to him, snuff about the lair's edges. Are they hiber-
nating? she asked when she joined him. Maybe not, he
told her. She examined the lair, looked around, commented: We're in the middle of nowhere.

Actually, Galen replied, we're almost there. Then he
stepped away, crossed the last of the ponds, ascended a
ridge and crossed its crest, dropped out of sight so suddenly that Jamie caught her breath sharply, felt her
throat constrict; and then she too cleared the ridge and
descended its sharp slope on the other side, which
evened out on the cusp of what she could have only
described as a cauldron-shaped field, an open, snow-
packed space that ended in a pine forest, and she walked
toward the pines, her ankles finally sore, her legs tired.
When she reached the forest's edge she saw Galen and
the dog but not the shack, at least not at first, because it
was hidden by trees pressing against it, the boughs

nestling its roof.

No one's been here, Galen told her, taking her knapsack from her shoulders. She stepped inside, saw the upright oildrum resting atop stones laid flat on the earthen floor, the square opening roughly cut out of the barrel's middle and the roughcut slit nearer its base, saw the short pipe thrust into its top leading to a hole in the roof. There's wood, she exclaimed in amazement, Galen behind her. I used to trap, he reminded her, in such a way that she found herself wondering whether he meant that he had stopped trapping or that he would never trap again, wondered the while as he put dried pine needles and pinecones and some twigs and then larger pieces of wood into the oildrum and struck a match, blew so that the fire caught, then took an oil lamp hanging from a hook on the wall and lit it too. The oil lamp and blaze dissipated the dimness. Galen retrieved a bucket from a corner and told her to fill it with snow—pack it down, he instructed—to melt for drinking water, told her to keep moving until the shack warmed, and then he brought their packs inside and took two snares and the ax, said: I'll be back.

The dog was already asleep near the fire when Galen returned without the snares and with armfuls of pine boughs. Jamie was melting snow, but then she stepped away, went outside so that he could move about the

cramped interior unhampered, arrange the boughs,
unroll the sleeping bags. She watched the night solidify
until Galen slipped past her, the aluminum pot in hand,
saying: You might want to get into dry clothes while I get
more snow. She went back into the warming shack then,
peeled off her jacket and sweater and shirt, pulled on
dry clothes and hung the damp ones on a nail, sat on a
sleeping bag and took off her boots and socks, peeled
the moleskin from her ankles. When Galen returned he
put more snow into the melting water, then set deer
meat to steaming in the aluminum pot. You'd better
change too, she told him, and he realized that she was
barefoot, that she would not leave the shack while he
changed, and turned his back to her. As he stripped
down to his waist, Jamie took in the shape of his shoulders, the smoothness of his skin, the fineness of his
arms, his back, and then he pulled on a sweatshirt,
another sweater. When he sat down on his sleeping
bag—like hers, atop a pile of boughs, but across from
her—Galen said: There's no sign of him.

I'm hungry, she replied.

Galen said nothing, once again astonished by her
living—deliriously—beyond whatever bounds he
understood to exist, living only from moment to
moment, not thinking of past or future or even any
reason for being here, as though she and the dog—and,

inadvertent as any mistake, he—were on this trek for no reason but the sake of the journey. The deer meat cooked, and he gave some to the dog. He and Jamie ate with their fingers, sitting cross-legged and almost knee-to-knee, facing one another. Their hands brushed once and Galen pulled back, unnerved, waited for her to take another piece and bring it to her mouth before he reached toward the pot again, for he distrusted himself, his senses heightened by the impression of her kiss and unruly with her closeness and the shack's smallness. When they finished he made broth from what was left, then tea when that was finished, and they drank both from a tin mug, sharing it, passing it between them, Galen tense with weariness from being too close to her, from that kiss, and relieved when she finally uncrossed her legs and pulled her knees up and wrapped her arms around them, rested a cheek on top of them, gazed at the dog and at the flaring oildrum and not at him. And then he moved away from her, pushed himself onto his sleeping bag, stretched out, put his hands behind his head, and willed his body to relax, give in, forget. Just as he began to fall asleep, she said in a quiet voice: So, Galen, if we're not going to make love, then tell me a story.

He tensed, opened his eyes. A story?

Your choice, she said, not taunting, not tempting,

but with finality.

I'm not sure I know any stories.

Tell me about Harlan.

And then you'll go to sleep.

And then I'll go to sleep.

He didn't move, breathe. And then he sighed, said: In the beginning, we were children—and she closed her eyes and saw herself small and alone in the scruffy yards behind the millworkers' housing—and we played in the cemetery where my mother was buried. The three of us: Bobby Sanders, Harlan, me. I don't remember being small without them. Bobby Sanders's old man always made pancakes for us, if it was early enough, if he wasn't too drunk, and we were always at Bobby's when we weren't at the cemetery or running wild somewhere else, because Harlan's place was misery, his parents always beating on one another or on him, and our place—until my father took on the animal farm—was just an apartment and a small one at that and in the middle of Goffston, and we had no use for Goffston. And then Bobby Sanders blinded himself one day, lost an eye, and his old man kept that eye in the cellar, which was piled high with everything and anything you could imagine and much of which you couldn't—he was some sort of amateur taxidermist, he had stuffed birds, beaver, weasels, fox, bear paws and bear heads down there, not to men-

tion fetuses he'd preserved, things he'd pulled from
pregnant kill that were mostly deformed, sometimes
two-headed or joined at the hip—and we'd play in that
cellar among all that stuff, the walls lined with shelves
and ogres, if it was raining and Bobby's old man had
passed out, which he did mostly every day and by
midday. But as we grew up, started to get older, that
place began to spook me, and I couldn't bring myself to
go over there as often, so that Harlan and Bobby were
more or less off on their own after a while. Without me.
And they got into a lot of trouble together, boys-will-be-
boys kind of trouble, until they began maiming and
killing pet cats and stray pups and rabbits and chickens,
Bobby wearing that patch over where his eye had been
and plucking out the eyes of anything he managed to get
his hands on, Harlan just going along, doing what
Bobby did and loving him the more for it, and me—
being left out—loving Harlan the more: you know how
children are, they have fantastic loyalties, bottomless
friendships. The two of them bonded the ways boys do
or maybe did then: they were blood brothers, something
deeper, closer than siblings, with me on the outside but
attached to Harlan the way Harlan was attached to
Bobby, and Bobby attached maybe to nobody but himself. I don't know. I saw a lot less of Bobby, and after my
father bought the animal farm, we lived out there every

summer, and I didn't see much of Harlan either. But
sometimes they'd ride out on their bicycles and we'd
have the run of the place, me watching Bobby squint
with his one eye at those deer and sheep, hens, goats, at
those ponies and ducks and geese, until I couldn't stand
seeing his longing to blind things: and then I'd end up
having to wrestle him to the ground, make him say
uncle, make him promise to leave the animals alone.
Harlan would just sit there watching, maybe just waiting
for the day Bobby would get the better of me. He never
did. By the time he could have, we were almost
teenagers, and Bobby had discovered that picking on
anyone weaker or smaller—girls and paperboys, kids
with glasses or braces, but never Harlan, who was
shorter and scrawnier than either of us, Bobby never
once touched Harlan—was more fun than torturing
animals. And so Bobby Sanders became the town bully.
As vicious and dull as any.

And Harlan? What was he?

Galen paused, answered: A clown. A prankster. Not
as tough as Bobby, and funnier, but maybe even back
then there was a mean streak in him Bobby brought out,
one I couldn't really see. Not even as we got older. By
then there were other things to notice. I mean, at one
point—I can't say when exactly—girls suddenly became
something else. Even Bobby took note of that. We

changed, and they changed. God, growing up was like falling off the edge of the world, over and again. You wake up one day and everything's different, sometimes terrifying, the world being neither how you remembered it the night before nor what you thought it was just yesterday. Bodies become mysterious, and my own was suddenly unbearable, unforgiving; summer heat made me crazy with longings, winter's cold inspired a horrible loneliness, there was an endless ache and pulse to things. To everything. As children who were once inseparable, we were no longer like that, each of us becoming weirdly unique and, faced with not being part of each other the way we'd been and being too young yet to be part of anyone else, we latched onto things, pretty much anything—dogs, cars, clothes, you name it—but pretty much nothing satisfied, nothing rubbed up against our souls, none of those things stroked us. And as we drifted further and further apart, some itch, some urge, some need took hold under the skin; for me, that itch urge need was to be someone else, to collapse into someone else, to be anyone but myself. Being yourself is the hardest thing in the world when you don't have the slightest idea of who you are. And it was awkward and terrible and basic—maybe primal—and unexpected, going from being children to being boys to being men and never ever having wanted to stop being children at all.

But it happened. And I pretty much became a loner, because even if I had no inkling of who I was—and I didn't—I happened to know who I wasn't. Harlan was still around, my only friend, and Bobby was mostly gone for me, except for Harlan's stories. I just about lived for those, and Harlan told me everything they did, the trouble they got into—the fistfights, the drinking, the car they stole from Bobby's old man whenever he'd pass out, the joyrides they took, the poaching they did, the collie dogs they sometimes strung up and skinned, the crazy girls they sometimes caught and laid: I heard all this and more, and maybe even envied them, certainly envied their skirt-chasing.

You didn't have a girlfriend.

Not then. I had Harlan's stories. It seemed easier, somehow, to live through them, at least while I was still in high school.

And later?

Later, Galen said. Later, there was someone, for a while. After I was drafted, when I was in the service, on my own—Bobby couldn't join up, and Harlan was rejected, probably because we weren't at war back then and the military wasn't yet in the habit of accepting anyone who couldn't read but had managed to cheat on his driving test—I had a girlfriend, for a while. Where I was stationed. But even then, I'd make my way back here whenever I got leave of any length, so that I could hang out with Harlan on the pretense of trying to teach him to track game no matter the season, just so I could listen to his stories. Which I couldn't get enough of, for they were hot, sinister, perverse. Because by that time, Bobby Sanders—or so Harlan put it—was in love.

Love, Galen repeated. What a mistaken notion, such fraud—and Jamie raised her head then, almost protested, stopped herself from going to Galen—for whatever Bobby Sanders felt or was even capable of feeling, it wasn't love. Until he met what he thought was his match, no female I knew of had put up for long with what went along with him—his wildness, his drinking, his violence, his cruelty, his need to dominate. And his match was a docile girl with too much flesh and so little understanding that Bobby couldn't even get a rise out of her, someone who did whatever he told her to do and who let him do anything to her he wished, *anything*. And that was his undoing. He couldn't get enough of her, and he couldn't stop himself. He did awful things and returned, over and over, to do them again. He'd buy her from her father, take her somewhere and keep her there until she figured out how to make her way back to her old man, the way a whipped dog always returns to where it's fed and beaten, and then Bobby would go after her again. Sometimes he and her old man would knock

her silly, and sometimes Bobby wanted him and Harlan
to watch, sometimes join in, until—if Harlan can be
believed—they were so exhausted that Harlan was able
to round Bobby up, drag him off. And that went on until
the day that girl's father figured he had something of
value on his hands, made sure enough men in Dyers
Corner knew about it, started parceling her out. When
Bobby got wind of that, he went crazy, and he and
Harlan went drinking, got drunk, started playing some
kind of spin-the-bottle with the kiss of death. Which
ended when Bobby put a gun to his head and pulled the
trigger.

Galen stopped speaking, lifted an arm, placed his
wrist over the bridge of his nose, his eyes.

And Harlan.

Harlan, Galen replied slowly, came undone. Not
that there was much left to undo.

And you?

No, not me. I came undone later, when Harlan got
me to go into the woods with Bobby's girl. Who didn't
even remember Bobby's name. Probably didn't even
remember him, know who he was. Or had been.

You went into the woods with her? Whatever for?

Galen made a muffled sound, cleared his throat. She
thought she was going on a picnic, he said. We—Harlan
and I—were supposed to go hunting. It was winter.

Harlan shot her dead. That's when I fell apart.

Jamie stirred, and then she was beside him, her hands light on his chest.

Don't, Galen said, please don't touch me. He took her by her wrists and put her hands in her lap, pushed away from her, settled onto his side with an elbow crooked and one hand under his ear, looked at her. His expression anguished.

I went to prison instead of Harlan, he told her.

I don't care.

Jamie—

I don't care. She reached out, but he clasped her hand in midair, halted it.

This isn't about whether you care or not, Galen said.

Then what is it? If it's not about your past, it's about mine—about Damon, who was never—

This is *not* about Damon. It's not even about my being an ex-con, or about the fact that Harlan thinks I'm taking revenge on him by hiding a boy he's after, a boy I've seen only once in the middle of the night, a boy I've never met. It's not about us being together here, where you can tell yourself that we just gave in to all this wilderness, gave in to the moment. This is about the fact that you will walk out of my life and into yours, and that I don't need to—no, I don't want to—have you or be had for memory's sake. I've got enough memories to last a lifetime. And I've already chosen to let you go.

What if I choose to stay.

You won't, can't.

Why not?

Because—and then Galen paused, for he was ashamed to admit what he was about to say—because, Jamie, there's nothing I can give you.

I never asked for anything. I'm not asking now.

He brought her hand down, placed it on her thigh, let it go. I know, he told her. That's how I knew you'd leave.

⌒

The scent of pine embers pungent and the shack cold, Jamie lay in her sleeping bag and listened to Galen's breathing, mulling over what Galen had said about refusing memory. Wondering if it were true, wondering whether memory could be something other than that which just occurs, the way she assumed everything that had befallen her had simply happened, for no discernible reason and even when hardly accidental the result of the same inevitability, and with as little reflection, as when a lightning rod accepts striking bolts; thinking too, for the first time, of the future as possibly being anything but some great void that was not so much ahead of her but all around her, as possibly being something that could be wrought, hammered into shape, determined, willed. As Margaret had once said to her, The amazing thing about human beings is that whenever they become conscious they're oh so liable to create their own existence. Although most humans resist that consciousness.

And then Jamie got up and without making a sound pulled on her boots and took her jacket and stole out the door, the dog on her heels. She made her way to the beaver ponds as the last of night pooled into day, trying to think with Galen's mind, feel with his emotions, see with his eyes. And she could not. She scanned their trail for any sign of disturbance—there was none—surveyed the mountains and sky for a sign, any sign, weighed the meaning of clouds, was incapable of imagining prison as anything more than a small room with bars on the windows having nothing to do with time, wondered if she were incapable of knowing what Galen thought love might be. Wondered too at whether what she felt when she kissed Galen might be love.

And then she slowly returned, found Galen gutting a rabbit that had been caught in one of his snares, watched him work deftly, throw the creature's entrails to the dog, cache the rabbit from a bough.

You should stay here, Galen told her, keep warm. I'll be back before nightfall.

Uh-uh.

The going will be rough. And it'll storm.

That's okay, she said. Then wrapped her own ankles
and rolled her sleeping bag and tied it to her repacked
knapsack, attached the snowshoes, set out behind him.
They tramped to where the trees became dwarfed and
sparse, and after the snow began to fall, soft as wet
goosedown and accumulating rapidly, they strapped on
their snowshoes, climbed higher. By midday they were
past the last of the treeline, and at one point she looked
up to see Galen and the dog paused side by side and
nothing else in the vast whiteness, neither sky nor
mountain nor the valleys below, and then they moved
on as one. She couldn't discern any trail or path, was
awed at being lost in a universe Galen alone comprehended in the way the blind know theirs, with a sense of
things undetected and unrealized by those who can see.
She felt insubstantial, exhilarated, made alive by nothing
but the feel of the slope under her and by not knowing,
not caring, whether that treacherous cliffside she
ascended would, on the other side, drop abruptly into
nothingness. When Galen called out to her, from far
ahead, she realized she could no longer see him, followed the sound of his voice, saw that he had taken off
his snowshoes. She did the same, climbed, caught up to
him. He scaled a bald reach, waited for her; and when
she asked for his hand he reached down, and she felt his

strength, the sureness of his grip as he pulled her safely onto the top. And then he broke his hold, let go first, and they stood shoulder to shoulder, close, as the dog pushed toward them, having found its own way to the top. Galen stooped, brushed the snowcake from its coat, said: We're almost there.

The shelter was only a cavern with a stone wall before it, and they sheltered within it, sat on the ground frozen beneath them. Galen pulled out some fried bread and gave two pieces to the dog and more to her, ate what was left.

No one's been up here, she commented, chewing thoughtfully.

Not for a long time, Galen replied grimly.

So.

So, we'll go back, tack down a different way, keep our eyes open. Not that we can see much.

We could spend the night here, she said.

We could, he agreed, but I'd prefer an oildrum fire and some rabbit for dinner. Besides, if the snow keeps up, we might get caught in a whiteout.

I wouldn't care.

I know, he told her, but I would. And then he got to his feet. Jamie walked by his side when the way allowed and kept to his pace from behind when it did not, the wind rising and becoming relentless, the snow closing in and blanching, erasing all. She began to feel cold, and they did not speak; nor did Galen ease into the comfort of her presence, for he didn't trust her to believe that certain things had been decided between them and certainly forever, was not serene despite that familiarity that demanded no words between them. When they finally reached the shack—gaping blacker than night—Galen abruptly, almost angrily, stepped out of his snowshoes and let her struggle out from under her knapsack, undo her own bindings, for he was unnerved by the echo of her intemperate, insistent *I wouldn't care*, by the thought of the night that stretched before them. And then she stepped inside the shack, shivering, frozen, stood by as he lit the oil lamp and kindled a fire in the drum before going out for snow and the cached rabbit The fire hissed and crackled and she stomped her feet, shivered the more, managed to get her sleeping bag unrolled and her boots off, crawled into the bag.

Galen, she said to him when he returned, I've never been so cold. Not even on your porch.

It took all the will he had to not do what he wanted to do, what she needed him to do: lie beside her, hold her just once and if only for once, warm her. He struggled with himself, silently cursed temptation and the impossible, thought of the fleshy, chest-blasted, motionless girl beside him, made himself say: I have.

And then he went to his backpack, pulled out the tobacco, rolled a cigarette, sat away from her. When the shack finally warmed Jamie climbed out of the sleeping bag, and they ate. She gave most of her food to the dog. They did not speak of tomorrow, or of the boy, did not speak at all, and when tomorrow came they walked into the phenomenal whiteout to make their solemn way back. She found herself thinking: This winter is endless.

〜

The fox paused but sensed no presence and thrust its nose into the snow and skimmed its surface as it trotted into the open, its magnificent tail linear with its back, the creature moving like a gaunt shock of copper through the densely snowbleached morn. Somewhere beyond the unseen and unseeable cloudcover the sun orbed, and for a fleeting moment a shaft of falling snow gleamed iridescent on a beam of diffused radiance through which the fox passed, nosing onward and unaware, hungrily intent upon finding mice and moles. Near the merry-go-round it suddenly froze, poised head up and with one foot tautly raised, every nerve in its body straining, and then the shot knocked it off its feet, rolled it in midair, the fox struggling even as it hit the ground to gain its footing and not being able to do so dying on its side, paws aquiver in phantom run.

Harlan lowered the rifle and spat, walked over to the creature and circled it though he knew it was dead, cursed his aim, the shot being too high—an almost-miss—for his liking, then toed the carcass and felt only death's resistance and so set to severing the tail with his blade, the blood splotching the snow. When he straightened, trophy in hand, he looked down at the maimed fox, spat again, looked up and cursed the uninhabited cabin, cursed Galen for having left and taken with him—wherever he'd gone—that girl and her mongrel and the boy, cursed Galen for having fooled and tampered with him, cursed himself for not having returned that same night after smacking the girl around, cursed himself for knowing that they'd lit out long before now, for the stovepipe that jutted from the roof wore a cap of pristine white that signaled no fire since at least the day before, and there were no footprints in the drive but his own. The kill, the season, the thought of Galen and that girl and her dog and the boy somewhere beyond his reach, the sight of that vacant cabin so infuriated Harlan that he dropped the foxtail and took a bead on one of the cabin windows, shot it out. He aimed again, shattered the other, and went to work on the door, sighting the lock and missing it and shooting again after walking closer, this time pinging metal. And then he stepped up onto the porch and butted the door open, walked into the cabin's empty cold and into its empty smell, an invader about to violate, raze all that remained as the reminder of everything that galled him.

Harlan destroyed the place. He smashed chairs and glasses and cups and plates and the vase, slashed the couch, tore the quilt from the wall and ripped it apart, knocked the contents from the cupboards, poured vinegar and molasses and ketchup and syrup on clothes and bedding and onto the floor, poured flour and water into the woodburning stove, shredded the shower curtain, knifed the mattress in the loft. He vandalized like a madman insane with drink, vandalized because he could and because what he ruined meant nothing and everything to him and because there was no end to that inbred violence within him no one could ever confuse with revelry; and Harlan took joy in his rampage as well as revenge, released some part of an endless rage that eventually led him back to retrieve the foxtail, made him reload his rifle and sight the carousel horses, take aim at their heads and manes, their hindquarters, their raised forelegs, and with the concentration of a serial sniper blast away. Thereafter Harlan stood still until the smell of gunpowder and hot metal dissipated, no longer tainted the pure scent of snow, then picked up the foxtail and left the way he had come. Never imagining that—and in actuality imagining nothing, not even

Galen's return, for Harlan was certain that Galen was gone, would no time soon look upon what Harlan had defiled—after finally reaching his truck and getting in and slamming the door, after pointing it in the direction of The Bend and driving into the whiteout, that the boy in the hunter's shack would raise his head at the sound of the truck's whine as it slowly passed by, as if straining to remember something, anything, beyond the walls, beyond the corner in which he sat, beyond his pain.

Twenty

The hunter looked up from notating nature's vagaries, brought the pencil to his mouth, saw the boy cock his head and listen intently, watched him struggle to his feet. The hunter ducked his head instinctively to hide the scar as the boy thumped his way along the walls, making noises unlike those of any human the hunter had ever heard, although he did not remember exactly the sounds he'd made after the deer's hooves ripped him open or the grief that spilled from him in cries when his brother died from the disease that had eaten into his bones and embedded in his brain and wasted him, a disease that had not been cured and could never have been cured by arsenic or mercury or any other poison Doc Buzzard had had on hand. No, the hunter could only compare the boy's noises with the torn snarling of a rabid dog and the bleat of a buck in rut, the boy snarling and bleating as he thumped the way with his good hand, pounded the walls, staggered about the shack by leaning into its periphery, butting and smacking his way around as he followed its shape.

His wound stank. Brutish streaks ran dark under his skin, from the discolored hand and wrist to the crook of his elbow. The hunter put the pencil down, read: *Sky unseen, blizzard conditions.* He thought to write, *Whether the boy understands language I cannot say,* changed his mind, considered that he had not chronicled his brother's illness. Considered too that he found himself inexplicably disturbed at having written almost nothing about the boy. Who, rallying in this frenzied and incomprehensible way, rattled the hunter, unsettled him, as did the fact that the boy had no name, or, if he did, the hunter did not know it. Which was as bad as being nameless, so far as the hunter was concerned, as bad as being less than any dog or horse or cat, certainly less than human.

Jordan, the hunter said, but the boy did not pause, perhaps did not even hear the hunter speak his dead brother's name, the name of a faraway river in a holy land so distant as to be, or so the hunter thought, unimaginable. Jordan, he repeated, to the same effect, knowing that the boy was failing, that the smell coming from him was the smell of death itself. The boy thrashed back to his corner and, like a bagged cat drowning, slid down into it. He floored himself, banged the back of his head against the wall. And then the hunter closed his journal carefully, smoothed its cover, remarked: I won't be able to bury you properly, without you having a name and what with the ground frozen solid, so I'd better get about saving you.

He stoked the stove and set a kettle of water on top of it, sat with his unscarred profile to the boy, waited for the kettle to sing. When it did, he poured the steaming liquid into a cup of molasses and whiskey, just enough to melt the molasses, knew the boy's raging thirst would tolerate even this. The hunter set the mug near to him on the floor, told him, Drink up.

The boy eventually reached for the mug. He spit out the first sip, took a second, gulped the rest, put the empty cup down and kicked it away. The hunter retrieved it, waited. When the boy's face went loose, the hunter refilled the mug and brought it over to him and this time placed it against the boy's lips. And the boy drank again. After the third cup, the boy hung his head, and his knees and elbows and wrists went limp. He opened and closed his mouth like a fish and gurgled, the sweat streaming down from under his hat.

The hunter was surprised by the boy's weight when he pulled him down onto the floor, laid him prone as a corpse. He heated the blade of a sharp knife on the stove top, waited for it to glow before dousing it with whiskey. The blade sizzled, and then the hunter went to the boy and crouched beside him, pulled the blackened edges of skin back from the gash in his hand, whittled away at the encrusted ooze, the leathery scabbing, the dark clots within the wound. The boy moaned, his eyes rolling beneath their closed lids. The hunter paused until the boy stilled, then sliced away strips of rot and nowhere found clean flesh, healthy flesh, even when blood began to smear the blade. Let it be, the hunter muttered, cutting a cross on the boy's palm, pressing at it with his fingers and watching foul-smelling pus burst to the surface. He rinsed the boy's hand with steaming water after that, the skin whitening around the wound's edges. A low scream came from deep inside the boy as he opened his eyes and, flailing his arms, drunkenly pushed himself away from the sopping mess and away from the hunter, drunkenly stared at his hand and what ran from it and emitted another ungodly wail.

The hunter dolloped bacon fat into a pan, let it bubble, mixed in a good portion of whiskey, approached the boy when he once again seemed to be unconscious. As he tilted the pan the boy came to, the pain of the burn terrible, and with a howl knocked it from the hunter's hand, splattering molten grease in every direction. The hunter backed off as the boy tried to rise. But he could not, instead drew his knees up as if to protect himself, glared at the hunter with unfocused lunatic eyes. The hunter then took a measure of whiskey for himself, downed it gratefully, and went out to feed his hounds.

Twenty-one

They had walked from the blind not in single file but beside one another and in Galen's unbroken steady rhythm despite her fatigue, and in the whiteout they grew accustomed to seeing only each other and the dog—sometimes pausing to shake itself free of the snow on its fur—the firs coming in and out of focus only as they passed, the emerging birch and maple and ash and oak thinned by snowcling. Their eyelashes and eyebrows were as white as their breath, their snowshoes heavy. Unspoken between Jamie and Galen was what both hoped, that this blizzard would keep Harlan away; unspoken between them too what they both knew, that nothing lasts forever and that when the blizzard ended so would their common purpose. Galen would return to his solitary life guarding more intensely than before the gates of his privacy, be mired in regret yet another layer deeper for her leaving; and Jamie would leave for nowhere, anywhere, both being the same, guarding nothing but the dog and learning if nothing else how to root regret. They came on through the snowstorm as though they were the only two on the planet, came on through the immediacy of the moment that had reduced them to bone and sinew and breath, broke out onto the knoll from which they could barely discern the merry-go-round and, exhausted, had no presence of mind to notice the dog ahead of them nosing at a mound where no mound had been. And then Galen slowed, stopped, caught at her arm, said *Oh jesus* in such a way that she looked up to see the dog frantically pawing at the mound of snow, and she cried out and began to run toward it despite the snowshoes, Galen trying to hold her back, telling her to stay where she was, the two of them forging forward and grabbing at each other the while, both fearing the worst, that under the mound lay the boy's frozen body.

They didn't notice the shattered wooden horses, could not yet see as far as the damaged cabin. They fell to their knees, pushed away the dog, dug with their hands, touched and saw the fur at the same moment. Jamie pulled her hands away then, Galen uncovering the fox, seeing the gunshot wound and missing tail, saying *Harlan* at the same moment she noticed the splintered carousel. When Galen saw that too, he pushed her down into the snow, put his mouth to her ear, told her to stay where she was, stay *down*, made her hold on to the dog before he pulled off his backpack and his snowshoes and got up, floundered toward the house at a crouch until he was close enough to see the shattered windows, the half-open door with its blasted latch and the snow drifting inside. His heart sank before he even reached the porch, because he knew the violation he would feel, the chaos he would find. Which he felt, found. Felt too his own reduction, belittling, losing to Harlan's incensed impulse not only what Galen owned, but all of his resolve, that resolve—to live in his own way, quietly, unobtrusively, sufficient unto himself, with all the dignity he had as much right to as anyone else—now contravened, wrecked, trampled. Galen walked into the cabin, walked out, went back to her and the dog with a crushed, bleak expression that brought her to her feet.

He dug out the fox alone, dragged its carcass toward one of the sheds, the dog circling him, as Jamie picked up Galen's snowshoes, went to the cabin, entered it, saw what Galen had seen, took off her knapsack and went back for his backpack and brought it onto the porch. And then she began where Galen could not, began because Galen could not. Jamie mucked out the half-solid, half-sodden flour from the woodburning stove,

cleaned out the stove's clogged insides, managed to
kindle a fire. She picked through everything strewn
about, separated into piles things unsalvageable from
those that weren't, picked up dented cans and any plates,
cups, glasses that weren't cracked or shattered, swept
away shards and spilled rice, scraped the coagulated
pools of ketchup, vinegar, molasses, and syrup from the
floor, mopped it down. Galen was not there, the dog not
there, and the blow came so hard through the windows
and open door that Jamie felt no hint of warmth even
after the stove began to blaze.

Galen gutted the fox in a shed, tossing its liver, heart,
kidneys, stomach onto the ground for the dog. The dog
hesitated, put its nose to the mess, finally nibbled deli-
cately at the fox's innards as if politely perturbed by
canine cannibalism. Galen watched, thought of his cellmate remarking: *They say it's a dog-eat-dog world but
I've never heard of or seen any dog eating another dog.
That's just people talking about themselves.* And then
Galen turned from watching the dog eat almost daintily,
hung the carcass from a hook, stood there because he
could not bear the thought of going back into the cabin,
stood there until he thought to do what he must: rip
siding from some stable or shed or leanto, handsaw that
siding into boards to nail over the windows, remain outside the cabin.

Which is what he did. He sawed to size and nailed
boards over the windows without once stepping inside,
without saying a word to her. When he finished he went
back to the stables and sheds, chose an old bolt lock and
wrangled it off a door, repaired as best he could the shattered cabin door, then had no choice but to affix the lock
from the inside. He stepped over the threshold, saw that
she had begun to burn pieces of the broken chairs, noted
that she'd placed the snowshoes against the wall where
the quilt had hung, thrown the unsoiled part of a
blanket she'd ripped in half over the slashed couch,
strung the rope he'd carried in his knapsack across the
room, was at the sink and about to wash out whatever it
was that Harlan had poured onto several shirts, saw too
that her knapsack remained packed. He secured the
lock, stood in the open doorway.

Galen, she said with her back to him, close it.

He bolted the door shut, remained there. When the
room warmed, he took off his jacket, went to where she
had put his backpack, rummaged in it for his tobacco,
rolled and lit a cigarette, went back to the door and
leaned against it, watched her. He blew smoke rings as
though he were bored, as though lounging against a
starboard rail on a tropical cruise because he was weary
of the sea, the ship, the blandness. And then he disgust-
edly crushed the cigarette underfoot, on the floor she

had washed.

You can't set this straight, he said.

She wrung out a shirt and turned, faced him, holding it before her as if she were naked and it her only modesty, as if unsure of what to do next.

Stop, Galen told her, just stop.

Why?

He opened his hands in a gesture of futility. Because it's useless to fix what can't be fixed.

I don't care.

Don't, he said, his tone remorseful, his voice breaking, *don't* tell me you don't care. This is *not* your place.

Jamie opened her hands, let the wet shirt go, carelessly let it drop onto the floor with defiance flaring in her eyes and in her battered face, in the way she tilted her chin and in the way she held herself as she walked in that magnificent way of hers, those shoulders impossibly square and she impossibly thin and her body somehow unyielding and fluid at once, the way she glided toward him with graceful resistance, with grace, despite the fact that her ankles were raw, her feet aching. She crossed the room. And then her arms were around his neck and her face was in the hollow of his shoulder, her breath on his neck.

Don't.

Hold me, Galen.

He tried to take her arms from about him. Her hands were in his hair and she lifted onto her toes so that her mouth was at his ear, then just under his ear, and then he was hanging on to her as though on to life itself, the sobs welling, coming explosively, until he had nothing left, was emptied of that grief that he feared would drip back into him, fill him again, because he was bereft of any future and had been brought back to the depths of his past. And then she extricated herself, took a step back, wiped gently at his face, kissed him, took him by the hand. They undid the sleeping bags that were still attached to their packs, unzipped both and layered one atop the other on the floor between the couch and the woodstove. She sat down and stretched out her hand, not in the way Galen had reached down to clasp her hand in the mountains—the way a hiker helps a companion cross a chasm or climb onto a ledge, a perfectly impersonal gesture—for there was no reserve to this moment, no aloofness between them. Galen had never felt so fragile, distraught. He let her take his hand, sat beside her. She turned his palm to the ceiling, studied it as though she were a fortune-teller, traced the lines on it, closed his fingers with hers.

It's time I asked you something.

Jamie—

Will you come with me?

Galen shook his head, aware of the boarded windows, the radiating heat, the hunger that hours ago started to gnaw at him. It's all wrong, he began, could not continue, his defenses and common sense shattered, and already that anguish for what might have been and would never be, that anguish born of knowing that if he refused her now he would never watch her before this cabin in a night of perfect moonglow, the undulating snow glimmering beyond her and the moonlight in her hair, dusting lightly her slender shoulders and silhouetting her chiseled thinness: already that anguish.

Galen, come with me, she said.

He shook his head again.

We'll go as far as we can, she told him, as far as we have to, until we can turn back. Come back.

Galen drew up his knees, clasped them, rested his forehead on them so as to not look at her. There's nothing, he finally managed to say, to come back to.

In the spring. Or summer. We'll come back then. I'll help with the cabin, the garden. You can start over again.

He raised his head, said: I'd lose you anyway—you'd pity me for as long as that, and then you'd leave.

Jamie took his face in her hands. No, she told him, you're wrong. Then I'd ask you for a horse.

～

Galen woke each time she stirred, held his breath, lay against the lankness of her body when she settled, held her, tasted her skin, smelled her hair, wondered at the sweetness of her mouth, at the infinity he had discovered within her. The cabin's warmth held, the dog dreamed dogdreams and whimpered.

They had not spoken of where they would go. He didn't care, for it no longer mattered: what mattered was to be with her. As soon as the weather allowed, they would go to Dyers Corner, where Galen intended to withdraw what money he could from his account, what was left of his father's life insurance policy, enough to hire someone to drive them elsewhere, where he could rent an apartment for them, find work, wait—as she said—for winter to break and—so Galen thought— evade fate by putting the boy and Harlan behind him. And if she said No, let's not stop here, let's not stop yet. Just come with me, he told himself that he would follow her toward where the sun rose or where it set, if that's what she wanted, because he would rather wander about in her footsteps than begin to envision how he might turn his back on her. And he told himself that the years separating them already meant nothing, that what was between them would not wear thin, never wane, was strong enough to bear the force of time passing. He told himself that if they were drawn back to this place in the spring, in the summer, if they started over, it would be because it was meant to be.

He told himself: She'll have a horse. Maybe two.

↬

Jamie kissed him awake. Galen opened his eyes and did not know whether it was dark or day outside, with the windows boarded, the lights out.

Say yes, she whispered.

He closed his eyes, sighed, teased: You're jailbait, Jamie.

Say yes.

Yes.

Twenty-two

His brain boiling silver bubbles threading upward and his arm on fire, on fire, the boy scooted about in the corner and got to his knees, smashed his forehead on the wall so as to splinter the pain, sent a shockwave through his skull and unsettled the bubbles, smashed his forehead again and knew it was good, saw streaks of light burst within his eyes. The hunter came toward him with an icy cloth and pushed the boy's hat off his head, lay the cloth on the boy's face, but the boy snarled and flung it off as though ridding himself of a veil, saw as though from a great distance the hunter who peered at the greenish-black river that spread along the boy's thin arm, coursing its way from his poisoned hand and pooling in his discolored veins just below the surface of his puffed, pustuled skin. The hunter stepped back when the boy arched his spine and threw himself forward,

smashed the wall again, and he left the rag on the floor
near where the boy sat stinking foully, went to the door
and opened it onto a world of snowbound stasis and
diaphanous light and cerulean skies, broke a path
through the windsculpted drifts to the dogpen and
back, noted the air's warmth, the already evident
snowmelt, thought to record *Temperatures springlike,*
clear skies, and fed the dogs, stood as they cavorted
around him while the boy crawled to the shack's
threshold and tumbled out, rolled about until he managed to bank himself in the snow and, listing, scoop at
it, pack it into his wounded hand and on his wrist and
forearm before noticing the hounds, the hunter, in the
pen. And then howled wolflike.

He's a goner, the hunter said aloud.

The hunter eventually wrestled the boy back inside,
pulled him back into the corner, set about making
breakfast. He put the frying pan on the woodburning
stove and spooned fat into it, glanced with averted face
at the boy staring around him openmouthed and seemingly without comprehension. I'm fixing us something
to eat, Jordan, the hunter told him, but the boy's eyes
registered nothing and the hunter waited for the fat to
sizzle and paid the boy no mind when he struggled to
his feet, stood for one moment swaying in the corner,
took one step, another, came toward him. You must be

hungry, the hunter remarked as the boy reached for the pan, grasped its handle.

The boy hit the hunter hard, the pan thudding against his skull. When the hunter caught the second blow he went down as though suddenly tired, sat on the floor, and with the third blow square atop his head slumped over, the boy weaving and muddled and with his brain boiling, boiling, dropping the skillet, losing his footing, his fall crunching the hunter's neck. And then the boy crawled back into the corner and sat smashing his head against the wall until splinters ate into his skull.

Some time later—though the boy did not know that any time at all had passed, knew nothing at all of time— he picked up the hat from the floor and pulled it low over his brow, breathed through his mouth, listened to the baying hounds. He crawled to the door on his hands and knees and got to his feet, staggered out, looked at his legs as though they were not his. Sensible of neither the uneven snow's depths and shallows nor the earth below, he stumbled off, blindly following the downward slope beyond the shack, leaving the hounds and their ruckus far behind.

Twenty-three

Galen watched Jamie, her back to him, pull on a T-shirt, a sweater over it, and slip into the jeans with the flag patched upside down on their backside. Margaret had called them Jamie's Fourth of July jeans, and Galen smiled to himself at the recollection, of Margaret telling him that Jamie had asked her whether she was going to Dyers Corner for the Bicentennial celebration, recounting that the question pushed what Margaret had termed all the wrong buttons. I said to her, Margaret told Galen, that wild horses could not drag me to celebrate any such thing, given that the founding fathers were undoubtedly not to mention rightly turning in their graves because they knew should they rise from the dead they wouldn't even recognize this country as the one they'd conceived, whose principles had been if not forgotten at the very least twisted and thwarted. For this

nation has wrecked far too many lives—I gave her Cuba
and the embargo, I gave her Chile and Allende, Argen-
tinean and Bolivian and Uruguayan dictators, half of
Central America, I gave her Vietnam and almost sixty
thousand Americans dead and three million dead Viet-
namese, I gave her Savak—and committed far too many
travesties in the name of fighting communism, the only
reference I made because I assumed she'd heard of it, for
me to stomach. No matter if, a couple of years ago, we
got rid of a criminal president—who was immediately
pardoned, so much for the concept of *and justice for all*
in a lawless land—nothing's changed. For somewhere
along the way we became a people with an attention
span about as long as my pinkie who developed a talent
for imperfect recall, which is as bad as no recall at all.
And all the while I'm ranting, she's perfectly composed,
not a hint of agreement or disagreement to her expression, nothing in her posture hints that I'm making her
uncomfortable, nothing to reveal I might be getting
through to her. So, in the end, assuming I'd assumed
incorrectly, assuming she'd never heard of Cuba or Chile
or even Vietnam, I told her that the flotillas and fire-
works in this feel-good spectacle were not going to grace
Dyers Corner anyway, which would have, at best, its cus-
tomary paltry parade of flagwavers. And, I added, no
floats. At which point, so composed as to almost be

indifferent, she said to me: I was just—that *just,* Margaret interjected—thinking it'd be nice to eat some hot dogs.

Galen had grinned then, shaken his head, asked: So, did you go with her?

Given that remark, Margaret told him, of course I did. And it was lovely, the best thing not being the parade, which she watched very attentively, or even the hot dogs, but the fact that she wore those jeans with that upside-down flag. Which didn't quite cause a stir but didn't go unnoticed either.

Jamie, Galen said. Margaret was fond of those jeans.

She turned around and looked down at herself, raised her eyes, smiled at Galen. Well, she told him, so am I.

You're ready to go

She nodded, her smile widening. You too.

Almost, he replied.

⤿

Galen boarded over the cabin door from the outside while Jamie and the dog waited, and then they trekked away from the cabin, the dog leading the way, sometimes pausing to look back at them as if to check their progress. Galen told Jamie only that they'd snowshoe the two miles to the road—which was, he reckoned, already plowed—then take them off, carry them to the hunter's place and leave them in his safekeeping, hitchhike and walk to Dyers Corner. Jamie laughed at the sunlight, squinted at the glare off the snow, sometimes raised a hand to her brow and shaded her eyes, exclaimed at the jays taking flight from snowladen branches hieroglyphed by their perch, their color that of the sky. She carried a sweater and two T-shirts in her knapsack, the only clothes she now had but for those on her back, broke through the snowdrifts beside Galen and held his hand despite the awkwardness of snowshoeing beside him, stole glances at his angular face, was glad of the smile that played at the corners of his mouth because of her attentions, was unaware that he was mostly lost in wondrous contemplation of this morning, last night, yesterday, the night before, of all that had happened since they'd spread those sleeping bags on the floor between the couch and woodburning stove. Of how it was to be together.

And then it appeared, just barely visible: the road, release. Jamie beamed at Galen when she saw it, knowing that it would take them to Dyers Corner and beyond, far from where her mother had been born, where her grandparents had lived and were buried, where Damon (so erased by Galen it was as though he had never been) now lived with his wife. She intended

for the road to take them far from Harlan and the boy—
who were already almost unreal to her, phantom people
she expected never to see again—and maybe even distance her from grief, leave her beyond the loss of her
mother and Margaret, who would in time become as
insubstantial as any wisp of dream. She had already forgotten the postmaster, would never know how he had
waited for her until exactly yesterday, when he discarded
an old shoebox filled with photographs, placed it into
The Four Corners' garbage bin before canceling her
mailbox (whose rental was overdue, unpaid); would
never know that the postmaster would, until the day he
died, remain haunted by the memory of Jamie's grandmother, who in the apparition of her granddaughter
one day appeared before him as substantial, in the flesh,
as though time had reversed itself with a cruel irony to
bring back the only woman he had ever loved, gave her
back her youth only to disguise her, dress her in those
castoff clothes he despised—the same threadbare work-
shirts, oversize T-shirts, baggy sweaters, bluejean jackets,
and bellbottoms worn by an entire generation in perfect
conformity, as though by unspoken agreement they'd
chosen to wear a uniform—and those clothes serving
their purpose, reminding him that the girl was not her
grandmother, just her spitting image and namesake.
And so was denied to him once again.

When Jamie and Galen got out of their snowshoes, Jamie put the leash on the dog, took her first unencumbered steps on the road, laughed as she slipped out of the past through some torn seam in the universe, slipped away from the interlude that had come between leaving her hometown and whatever would come now, stepped into the future with Galen and let him lead the way. They heard the hounds long before they neared the hunter's shack, the dogsong distant, melancholy, sonorous, becoming more distinct, distressed, as they drew closer. Galen finally stopped, turned to look at her, his expression quizzical. He frowned slightly as he listened, stated: Something's wrong.

⌐

Harlan—in a foul mood, having been called a worthless cocksucker by the junkman and worse by Ada when he finally admitted (after plowing their drive, and that rankled) he'd lost track of the boy, of that girl and her mutt, of Galen—pounded the wheel as he drove aimlessly about at dangerous speed. He caught sight of the buck in the corner of his eye as he passed it, braked hard into a curve, and even as the pickup's tailend swerved glanced at the rearview mirror to see the deer leap across the road behind him, gather its haunches and clear the embankment, vanish into the woods.

Harlan threw the gear into reverse and backed up, pulled over to the side of the road and brought the pickup to a stop, cut the engine. He reached for his rifle and was out the door in one motion, walked to where the buck had cleared the snowbank and climbed over that, some yards on stood still, held his breath, peered into the woods, listened. And then he saw it: amber. Amber between gray and black, between boulder and treetrunk, enough amber to warrant a shot. Harlan raised the rifle, sighted the amber patch, and pulled the trigger, the rifle kicking into his shoulder and the amber, the deer, disappearing, disappeared. He heard thrashing, then nothing, hurried over to where the buck had been when he shot it, saw the vermilion splotches staining the snow, knew the deer was so badly wounded that it would eventually become exhausted, drop. He cursed the snow's uneven depth, the going that would be all downhill—which meant the dragging would be all uphill—and went on, toward the reservoir, in the buck's tracks.

⤳

Galen fought back his anxiety as they approached the hunter's shack, tried to betray nothing of his unease, pretended calm even after Jamie's dog became so unruly, intractable, that it took all the strength she had to hold it back. The hounds' mournful howling was ceaseless. And then they saw the pen, the wildly inconsolable dogs, the shack with its door wide open, no sign of the hunter.

Galen halted, told Jamie to wait, to keep the dog on a tight lead, and he took both pair of snowshoes and walked into the hunter's yard, glancing back once to see that she'd managed to make the dog sit, was holding it by the collar as well as the leash. As Galen drew nearer the shack, he spoke to the hounds to calm them and to no avail, then called out the hunter's name over that canine cacophony, went to the threshold. A stifling wave of heat greeted him, and as Galen's eyes adjusted to the dim interior he made out the table, chairs, stove, before the shock hit him, made his breath implode, explode. He dropped the snowshoes and without realizing he'd moved at all found himself kneeling beside the hunter's crumpled form, the purplish scar on the hunter's face darker than it had ever been and the hunter's eyes glazed, his bashed skull leaking.

Galen retched, staggered to his feet. He stood shakily, not knowing what to do and knowing too that there was nothing he could do. When Jamie called his name, Galen stumbled to the doorway and steadied himself with one hand on its frame, could not find his voice. The hounds leaped crazily, pushed off the fencing, bayed. When Jamie stepped over the snowbank, her dog tried to break away from her with an almost-human whoof, dragged her to her knees in the snow so that she pulled the creature back to her and unleashed it, Galen unable to cry out *No, no, no.* He put a hand up as if to halt traffic, but the dog raced past him and Jamie came toward him, kept coming, so that the only thing he could do to stop her was to run at her. He almost tackled her, lifted her off her feet, held her tight to keep her from the hunter's place, but his silence, his grip, panicked her so that she flailed at him, tried to break his hold by pounding his arm, kicking her way free, screaming, *What's wrong? What's wrong?* And then he heard himself over the din, his voice strange, his words frantic: Call the dog, Jamie. *Call the dog back.*

What's happened? she cried, not struggling against him, not struggling now. Where's the —

Just call the dog. Galen released her, ripped off his backpack, grabbed for Jamie's knapsack and began wresting it from her shoulders, his face wild. Jamie looked at him as though he'd lost his mind, and then sloughed off the knapsack, let it drop, yelled the dog's name, yelled again.

Bring the leash, Galen said, his voice still strange, frantic, and he grabbed her jacket sleeve and tugged—for he did not want her to go into that shack, did not want her to see—pulled her away, hurrying, stumbling through the uneven snow, trying to fly in the boy's wake, pushing through the drifts and sometimes sinking up to his thighs, pressing on. Jamie struggled to keep up with Galen's frenzied pace, finally wrenched her arm free so that she could follow him without falling. Galen plunged on, repeatedly calling out the dog's name, with Jamie behind him, the slope steepening and the snowdepth varying, sometimes lessening, until they were almost at the reservoir's edge where, breathless, imbalanced, Jamie tripped and sprawled facedown, picked herself up, and at that instant saw it: the windswept lake's glaring expanse, the outcrop Galen was already on, kicking at the snow, clearing the snow away. An inhuman sound tore from her: this was it, this the place, nowhere near where she imagined it might have been and nothing to it at all now that there was no possibility of pilgrimage in remembrance of her mother, of a day in their lives. And then she was at the outcrop's base, Galen reaching for her, clasping her wrist, pulling her up, putting his mouth to her ear and saying in his strange, frantic voice: *Whistle, Jamie, call the dog. Get the dog to come.*

He shook her, so that she did what he said, brought her trembling hands to her mouth, whistled with her fingers two long, loud notes, whistled again, barely able to see through a film of tears the boy on the ice and the

dog closing in on him, both far from beyond a low
promontory lined with abandoned bobhouses. And
then Galen was gone, no longer on the outcrop but on
the snowrippled shoreline, then on the ice too, cutting a
diagonal toward wherever it was he assumed the boy
and dog were heading. Jamie wiped at her eyes and
fought back a sob, yelled the dog's name once, twice,
whistled again and saw the dog pause, turn, stare in her
direction. She tried to whistle again, her hands shaking
and her lips, mouth, too dry, cried out the dog's name
again, the dog still unmoving until paying attention to
her this time and leaving off the chase, beginning to
head back as Galen passed it. Jamie scrambled down
from where she stood, rushed toward the shore and
toward the dog as it came at her, Jamie terrified by that
curious solidity below the snow that rimmed the reservoir's shore, terrified at being on the lake's surface,
watching with double vision the dog and Galen, and
Galen far—now on sheer, windswept ice—from her and
gaining on the point at which he thought he could inter-
cept the boy, knock him down, knock him out, do anything necessary to stop him.

The dog flew at Jamie, almost flew by her, but she
lunged, caught at it, yelled *Stay* and leashed it, then
began to pull the dog toward the shore. She could not
stop saying *Faster, faster,* could do nothing but keep her

eyes on the way, could not look back until she and the
dog were on the sloped bank of deeper snow under
which was solid earth; and only then did she look back,
see that Galen and the boy were almost at the edge of a
long finger of open water that blackly split the reservoir's dazzling whiteness. *Come,* she cried breathlessly at
the dog, *come,* and the dog bounded through the snow
at her side as she gained the back of the outcrop, circled
it until finding a way they could both climb it, the dog
losing its balance once and clawing back, scrambling to
the top.

Galen and the boy were near collision and nearly at
that strand of open water when the buck emerged from
the forest, staggered past the bobhouses and reached the
earth's end, gathered itself and leaped onto the reservoir's surface, went down splaylegged and struggling to
get its hindquarters and forelegs beneath it, heaved itself
upright and lowered its head and stumbled into a blind
trot, bleating, dripping and coughing blood, weaving
toward Galen, the boy, that black water as if pulled
toward all three by some invisible towline. And Jamie
gasped to see the deer, to see Galen reach the boy and
grab him, swing him around so that the boy fell on his
back, stand over him. She could not tell that Galen's
breath came ragged and hard, could not know how
pallid the boy was beneath him, how ghastly the boy's

hand and how perfectly expressionless, colorless, death-
like, his eyes. Galen gulped at the air, pulled the boy to
his feet, caught him under his arms when he wobbled,
crashed sideways with him and held onto him anyway
even as Galen got to his knees and back onto his feet and
as the wounded buck continued toward them in that
exhausted, stumbling trot. And then the deer stopped,
not distant from them—so close that Galen within
twenty steps could have reached out and touched it—
raised its head high, looked over its shoulder.

Nooooooo, Jamie screamed.

The shot lifted the deer's hind and propelled it forward and then onto its side, and her cry lingered in the
air for as long as it took for Galen to drop the boy, step
away from him. Jamie's chest seized and blood pounded
in her ears, and she saw the stilled figures at variant
angles upon the snow, the ice, saw the reservoir's glaring
vastness and that dark streak of open water with its
pearl-hued edges, saw with great clarity the boy hold up
one crooked arm as he lay on his back and the buck's
tilted rack of horns as it lay on its side, saw Galen
motionless, Harlan walking toward the deer. When
Galen took a step in Harlan's direction, raised his hand,
signaled stop, the deer inexplicably came to life, moved
at the same instant, somehow got to its feet and limped
forward, one hind leg dragging uselessly, its head down,

and then she saw Galen wave both arms, as if to warn off the buck, wave off Harlan. The deer crumpled with the second shot that severed its spine, its legs folding under it and crashing onto its belly, again rolling onto its side and this time stilled forever.

Nooooooo, Jamie screamed again. In the distance, Galen turned to look in her direction, saw her and the dog atop the outcrop before he whirled, sprang at the boy who was up and passing him by, heading toward the deer. Jamie heard Harlan yell something she could not understand, saw Galen freeze and the boy suddenly stop, lift his arms as if they were wings and, raising his face heavenward, turn one circle, another, spinning the world around him and moving from foot to foot with delicate precision, performing imperfect pirouettes but pirouettes nonetheless, spinning the world before him and not knowing when or whether one last turn would spin him from life. When the bullet hit him, whirled the boy into his final revolution before he dropped, she heard Galen scream. He screamed as Harlan ambled over to the deer and put a bullet into its brain, and he continued to scream even after he reached the boy and fell to his knees, pulled off his jacket, pressed it to the boy's chest, screamed kneeling by the boy's body as Harlan sauntered away from the deer and made his deliberate way toward Galen and the prostrate boy.

Harlan shouting once—this, Jamie heard distinctly—
Shut up, shut up, just before Galen got to his feet and
went for him.

Jamie could not have heard the thud when Harlan
brought the rifle butt down on the side of Galen's face,
but the sound went through her. And then all sounds
but those tearing from her died, Harlan standing silent
and looking in her direction, the deer and boy and
Galen prone and motionless and silent, the reservoir
lording silently over what had once been the valley, the
ice and reservoir waters silent above those homes in
which Jamie's grandparents and the postmaster and
others had once lived and those places wherein they had
once interred their dead, silent as the dreams the reservoir itself had once displaced and then drowned, the boy
and deer and Galen wasted upon a frozen wasteland of
unremitting silence. The dog whined, the only sound to
be heard until a great whiplash crack reverberated and
the ice fissured, splintered, caved in.

Nooooooo.

⌐

The boy heard it, heard that thunderous crack—
more deafening than the one that had knocked him off
his feet—and thought he was still spinning a circle, for
before him the horizon turned and before him a prone

deer and one prone figure and another figure standing upright, shadowing darkly, reeled; and when the boy went down, slow-spiraled downward, his hand wrist arm no longer burned and his brain no longer boiled and those hands pressing into his chest were no more, the heaviness gone. He was weightless, whirling, free, and there was nothing for him to distinguish, comprehend, no dull thuds or thumps, no ear-splitting cracks, and so he distinguished, comprehended nothing and was neither surprised by nor curious at the tickle in his throat that bubbled into his mouth and burst from him in a welt of liquid warmth, neither astonished nor unastonished that his eyes veiled with blood through which he could see, saw, crimsoned ragtag children milling around but away from where he was tied to a tree, their bodies shadowing phantomlike on the rose-tinted road and stranger yet the dog's flaming eyes and the iridescent hands of the girl who spirited him from the snake-like embrace of the rope; and as the fetters fell away, something like wildfire surged within him, even his eyes burned as he slid down the tree's trunk and into the cool, cold, frigid waters. The boy breathed in, greedily gulped the waters closing over him, its liquid freeze extinguishing all heat and then the pull of it heavy, heavier, the color of it dark, darkening, graying the jagged shapes of the floes above in the way night shades the clouds. Someone sank serenely beyond him, and someone else followed, twisting slightly as if twirling in a current. A deer slow-tumbled downward, passed close to him, its antlered head lolling. And the boy felt himself laughing, laughing, to see such a sight.

Twenty-four

The starkwhite floes and black waters closed over Galen, the boy, Harlan, the deer, and they disappeared as though they had never been, slipping voiceless and unstruggling below the surface, into the deep that covered the valley's past. The ice rearranged itself into unjoined pieces of a puzzle as Jamie crawled down from the granite outcrop she had once come in search of, the sounds that tore from her rending the silence. She crawled on her hands and knees, leashed to a dog that was now and once again all she had, to the reservoir's edge, and there she tried to stand only to have her knees buckle. She fell backward, the dog still leashed to her, and sat, wailing, keening; and from where she sat, wailed, keened, she was unable to see the deer inexplicably bob to the surface, float for an instant, two, then sink again, far beyond that promontory where—near a handful of bones, all that remained of a child's animal-gnawed carcass—bobhouses stood sentinel, bearing witness to what they could never reveal. Jamie sat near the reservoir's edge, with the dog beside her, where she railed and wept, keened and grieved, and did so inconsolably. In the manner of her grandmother, to whom she bore great resemblance.